THE
UNDERTAKER'S
DAUGHTER
by Jolene Skvarek

Copyright © 2026 Vivifica Studios

All rights reserved.

ISBN: 979-8-9933345-1-6

# The Teashop Murders

# The Gilded Corpse

Ashes
in the
Tenement
Chapter 1 183
Chapter 2 195
Chapter 3 205
Chapter 4 215
Chapter 5 225
Chapter 6 233

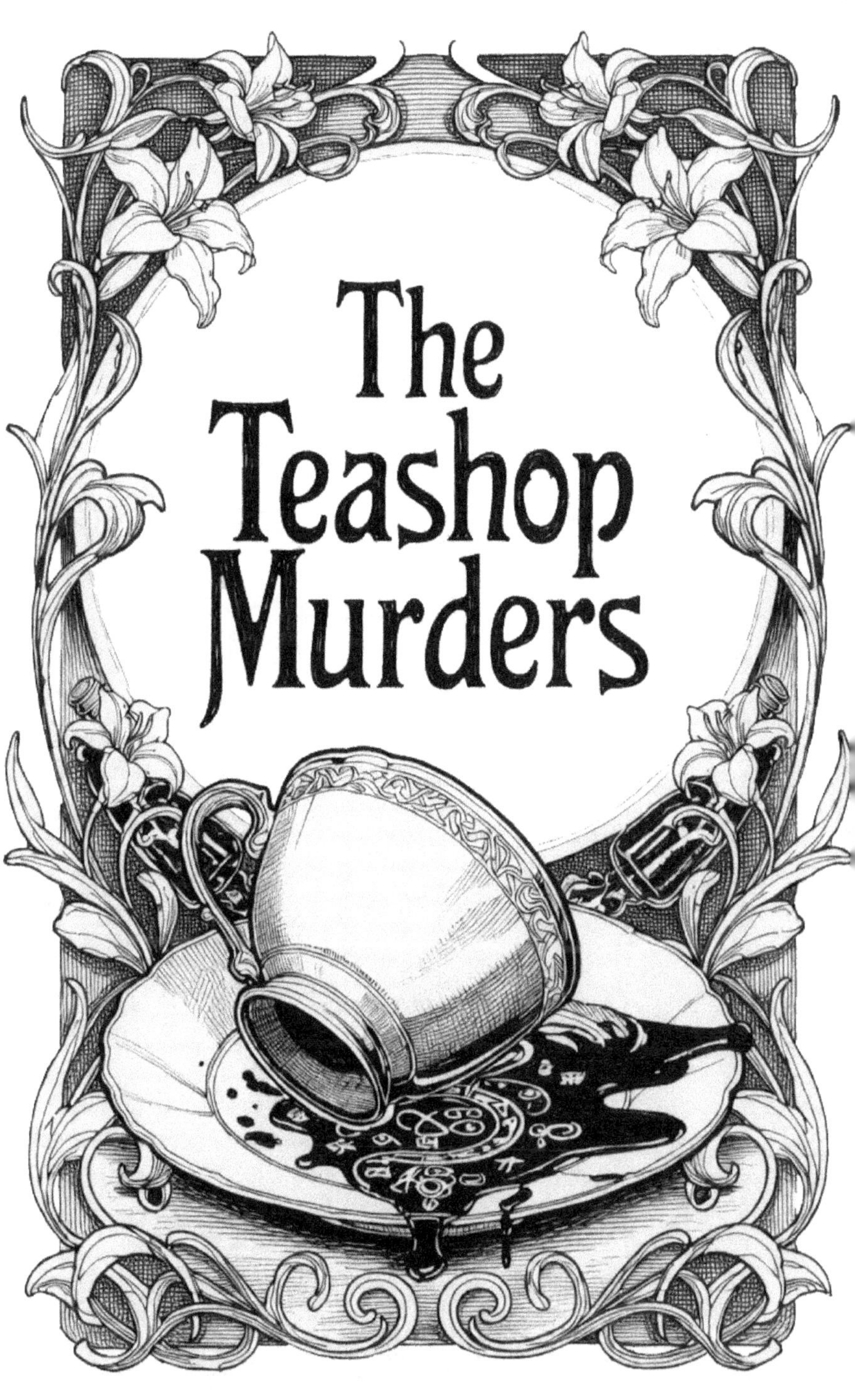
The
Teashop
Murders

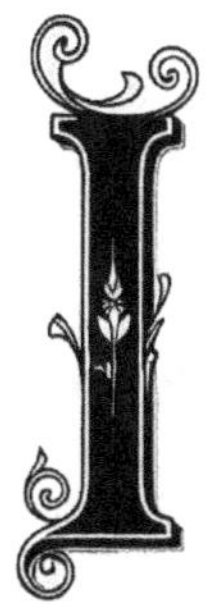

The dead, Lillian Cross had learned, were terrible gossips. She adjusted the oil lamp's wick, casting steadier light across the marble preparation table where Mrs. Catherine Henley lay in eternal repose. Or what passed for repose, the woman's face bore the pinched expression of someone who'd spent her final moments deeply annoyed. Given that Mrs. Henley had expired while berating a shop clerk over the price of silk ribbons, Lillian supposed the expression was fitting.

"What secrets are you keeping?" she murmured, dipping her pen in ink to sketch the deceased woman's features in her leather-bound notebook.

The authorities had ruled it a sudden apoplexy, the heart simply giving out, but something about the blue tinge around Mrs. Henley's lips nagged at her.

The basement of Cross & Sons Funeral Parlor

hummed with the sounds of a city that never quite slept. Above her head, the elevated train rattled past with its cargo of late-shift workers and ne'er-do-wells. Through the small street-level windows, gaslight flickered against the October fog rolling in from the East River.

"Lillian, dear, are you sketching corpses again?"

She didn't look up from her work.

"Good evening, Father. And they're called anatomical studies."

Edmund Cross descended the narrow stairs, his footsteps measured and careful. Twenty-three years in the mortuary business had taught him to move like a shadow, quiet, unobtrusive, respectful of the dead and their grieving families.

"Anatomical studies," he repeated, settling his wire-rimmed spectacles to peer over her shoulder.

"Is that what we're calling your morbid fascination with forensic details?"

"There's nothing morbid about curiosity." Lillian added another careful line to capture the peculiar discoloration she'd noticed.

"Mrs. Henley didn't die of apoplexy."

Edmund sighed, the sound heavy with paternal concern.

"The physician signed the death certificate. The family has made their peace with sudden heart failure."

"The family wants their inheritance settled quickly."

Lillian set down her pen and turned to face her father. At fifty-two, Edmund Cross looked older than his years, gray threading through his dark hair, lines etched deep around his kind eyes. The weight of other people's grief had a way of settling into a man's bones. "But look at this."

She lifted Mrs. Henley's upper lip with a pair of tweezers, revealing the gums.

"See this blue-black staining? And the way it's concentrated here, along the gum line?"

"I see a woman who died of natural causes," Edmund said firmly. "As the physician determined."

"A physician who spent all of three minutes examining the body and was more interested in his pocket watch than his patient."

Lillian pulled out her magnifying glass, a gift from her father on her twentieth birthday, though she suspected he now regretted encouraging her investigative tendencies.

"This staining pattern suggests poisoning. Something metallic, administered over time."

"Lillian."

The warning in his voice was clear, but she pressed on.

"Lead, perhaps. Or mercury. It would explain the sudden collapse—"

"Enough." Edmund's hand closed gently over her wrist, lowering the magnifying glass.

"We prepare the dead for burial, my dear. We don't investigate their deaths. That's not our place."

Lillian studied her father's weathered face, seeing the familiar tension there. She knew the careful balance he maintained—treating rich and poor with equal dignity while navigating the delicate politics of Manhattan society. The wealthy families expected discretion above all else. Questions, especially the sort Lillian favored, were bad for business.

"Of course, Father," she said finally, though they both knew she was merely agreeing to disagree.

A sharp rap echoed from upstairs, followed by the jangle of the front door bell. Edmund glanced toward the ceiling with a frown.

"Expecting anyone?" Lillian asked.

"Not at this hour." He checked his pocket watch, nearly eleven o'clock. "Stay here."

But Lillian was already untying her leather apron, curiosity winning over obedience as usual. She followed her father upstairs, emerging into the more genteel parlor where families came to make arrangements. Gas fixtures cast warm light over burgundy wallpaper and comfortable chairs designed to ease the burden of grief.

Through the frosted glass of the front door, she could make out two figures, one tall and broad-shouldered, the other slight and feminine. Edmund opened the door, and cold October air swept into the parlor along with the visitors.

"Mr. Cross? I'm Detective Nathaniel Blackwood, Metropolitan Police."

The man's Irish accent was unmistakable, though he'd clearly worked to soften its edges. He was younger than Lillian had expected, perhaps thirty, with dark hair that needed cutting and intelligent green eyes that seemed to catalog every detail of the room. His coat had seen better days, and his boots bore the mud of tenement streets.

Beside him stood a small, elegant woman wrapped in a black wool cloak. Even in the gaslight, her Asian features were striking, high cheekbones, dark eyes that missed nothing, silver threading through her black hair despite her apparent youth.

"This is Miss Evelina Cho," Detective Blackwood continued. "There's been a death at her establishment. Sudden and… suspicious circumstances."

Lillian stepped forward before her father could respond.

"What sort of death?"

Blackwood's eyes fixed on her with obvious disapproval.

"And you are?"

"Lillian Cross. I assist my father with preparations." She kept her voice level, though something about the detective's dismissive tone irritated her.

"What were the circumstances?"

"Miss Cross," her father said quietly, "perhaps you should—"

"A woman collapsed in my tea shop this afternoon," Miss Cho interrupted, her voice carrying only the faintest accent.

"Mrs. Vivian Ashworth. She was taking tea when she suddenly... convulsed. The physician believes it was her heart, but…"

"But?" Lillian prompted. Miss Cho's dark eyes met hers.

"There were… peculiarities. Things that didn't seem natural." Miss Cho said. Detective Blackwood shot his companion a sharp look.

"What Miss Cho means is that we'd like your professional opinion on the deceased before we release the body to the family."

Edmund cleared his throat. "Of course, Detective. We'll be happy to assist the police in any way we can."

"Excellent." Blackwood glanced around the parlor with poorly concealed disdain.

"I assume you have facilities for examination?"

"Naturally." Edmund gestured toward the basement stairs. "If you'll follow me."

As the group moved toward the basement, Lillian caught Miss Cho's arm gently. "These peculiarities you mentioned, what exactly did you observe?"

The tea shop owner glanced toward the two men descending the stairs, then leaned closer to Lillian.

"The teacup," she whispered. "The pattern of stains it left on the saucer, they weren't random."

"What do you mean?"

Miss Cho's expression was troubled. "I mean

someone wanted Mrs. Ashworth dead, Miss Cross. And they used my establishment to do it." Before Lillian could respond, Detective Blackwood's voice echoed up from the basement.

"Miss Cross! If you're quite finished gossiping, we have a body that needs examining."

Lillian exchanged a meaningful look with Miss Cho, then called down, "Coming, Detective. Wouldn't want to keep the dead waiting."

As she descended into her domain, the basement kingdom where she'd learned to read the stories written in flesh and bones, Lillian felt the familiar thrill of a puzzle taking shape. Mrs. Ashworth's death might have appeared natural to the authorities, but she suspected the truth would prove far more interesting.

After all, the dead were terrible gossips. You just had to know how to listen.

The gaslight cast dancing shadows across Mrs. Vivian Ashworth's face as Lillian arranged her examination tools on the small side table. The woman had been beautiful once, high cheekbones, delicate features, silver-blonde hair still elegantly arranged despite her ordeal. But death had leached the color from her skin, leaving behind a porcelain mask that reminded Lillian uncomfortably of the expensive dolls in Fifth Avenue shop windows.

"She collapsed around three o'clock," Detective Blackwood said, pulling out a small notebook and consulting his cramped handwriting. "According to witnesses, she was taking afternoon tea with two other ladies when she suddenly gasped, clutched her chest, and fell forward onto the table."

"The other ladies?" Lillian asked, carefully lifting Mrs. Ashworth's eyelids to examine the pupils.

"Mrs. Eleanor Hartwell and Miss Constance Blackwell. Both society matrons, both properly horrified. They've given statements." Blackwood's tone suggested he found society matrons about as useful as ornamental furniture.

Lillian glanced up from her examination. "And you believed them?"

"Why wouldn't I? They had no reason to lie."

"Everyone has reasons to lie, Detective. The question is whether those reasons outweigh their fear of getting caught."

Edmund cleared his throat diplomatically. "What did the attending physician determine?"

"Dr. Morrison examined the body at the scene," Miss Cho answered. "He pronounced it heart failure and signed the death certificate within minutes."

"Dr. Morrison," Lillian's voice carried a note of distaste. "Let me guess, elderly, well-connected, and more concerned with his social calendar than his medical duties?"

Blackwood's jaw tightened. "He's a respected physician with forty years of experience."

"Forty years of looking the other way when wealthy families prefer convenient diagnoses." Lillian returned her attention to Mrs. Ashworth, running her magnifying glass along the woman's neck and arms. "Miss Cho, you mentioned peculiarities. What exactly did you observe?"

The tea shop owner moved closer, her dark eyes intent on the body. "Mrs. Ashworth arrived alone, which was unusual. She typically came with friends. She seemed… agitated. Kept checking the door as if expecting someone."

"Or afraid someone might arrive," Lillian murmured, noting a small puncture wound behind Mrs. Ashworth's left ear, nearly hidden by her carefully arranged hair. "Detective, bring that lamp closer."

Blackwood obliged, though his expression remained skeptical. "What are you looking for?"

"Evidence." Lillian adjusted her magnifying glass, studying the tiny wound. "This puncture is fresh, made within hours of death. See how clean the edges are? This wasn't made by falling onto the table."

"Could be from a hairpin," Blackwood suggested. "Women wear enough of them to armor a cavalry unit."

"Hairpins don't penetrate this deeply. And they certainly don't leave traces of foreign substance." Lillian scraped a tiny sample from around the wound with her scalpel, transferring it to a glass slide. "Father, may I borrow your microscope?"

Edmund hesitated, then nodded toward the corner where his prized Zeiss microscope sat on a sturdy table. "Be careful with it."

As Lillian prepared her slide, Miss Cho spoke quietly to Detective Blackwood. "There was something else. After Mrs. Ashworth collapsed, I noticed her teacup had fallen in a very specific pattern."

"Meaning?"

"The tea stains on the saucer, they formed marks. Deliberate marks."

Blackwood rubbed his temples, looking like a man fighting a headache. "You're suggesting someone murdered Mrs. Ashworth and then… what, left coded messages in tea stains?"

"I'm suggesting," Miss Cho said calmly, "that you should examine all the evidence before dismissing it."

Lillian looked up from the microscope, her pulse quickening. "Detective, you need to see this."

Reluctantly, Blackwood approached the microscope. "What am I looking at?"

"Crystalline residue. Consistent with an alkaloid compound, possibly strychnine or a similar poison."

Lillian stepped back to give him room. "Someone injected Mrs. Ashworth with a lethal dose, probably using a hypodermic needle."

Blackwood peered through the eyepiece, his expression growing more serious. "This could be contamination from the embalming process."

"We haven't begun embalming," Edmund said quietly. "And we don't use alkaloid compounds in our preservation methods."

"Furthermore," Lillian continued, "the injection site behind the ear suggests someone with medical knowledge. It's a location that would be easily concealed by hair, and the jugular vein runs close to the surface there. A small dose directly into the bloodstream would act within minutes."

Detective Blackwood straightened, his earlier dismissiveness replaced by sharp attention. "You're saying this was a professional killing."

"I'm saying someone wanted Mrs. Ashworth dead and had the knowledge and tools to accomplish it quickly and quietly." Lillian cleaned her magnifying glass with a soft cloth. "The question is why someone would murder a society matron in broad daylight in a respectable tea shop."

"Maybe she wasn't as respectable as she appeared," Miss Cho said softly.

All eyes turned to her. "What do you mean?" Lillian asked.

Miss Cho glanced toward the basement stairs, as if checking for eavesdroppers. "Mrs. Ashworth visited my shop regularly, but never for tea. She came for… information."

"What sort of information?" Blackwood squinted his eyes at the woman.

"The kind that wealthy ladies pay handsomely to obtain. Who's having affairs, who's lost money in bad investments, which families are facing scandal." Miss

Cho's expression was carefully neutral. "She was what you might call a collector of secrets."

Detective Blackwood pulled out his notebook again. "Are you telling me you run some sort of gossip exchange?"

"I run a tea shop, Detective. But Manhattan society is a small world, and people talk. Mrs. Ashworth simply paid attention to what they said."

Lillian studied the tea shop owner with new interest. There was more to Miss Cho than met the eye, the careful way she chose her words, the sharp intelligence in her dark eyes, the expensive cut of her clothing despite her modest profession.

"Who else knew about Mrs. Ashworth's... collecting?" Lillian asked.

"Anyone who had secrets worth hiding," Miss Cho replied. "Which, in my experience, includes most of Manhattan's elite."

Edmund had been listening in increasingly uncomfortable silence. "Detective Blackwood, if this is indeed a murder investigation, perhaps we should contact the proper authorities."

"I *am* the proper authorities," Blackwood said sharply. "At least until someone decides this case is too important for an Irish cop from the Lower East Side. The bitterness in his voice was unmistakable, and Lillian felt a unexpected surge of sympathy. She recognized the frustration of being dismissed because of circumstances beyond one's control.

"Then we'd better solve it quickly," she said, "before someone else decides to interfere."

Blackwood's green eyes met hers, and for a moment, the antagonism between them shifted into something like understanding.

"Miss Cross," he said slowly, "I get the distinct impression you're about to suggest something that will complicate my investigation considerably."

Lillian smiled, the first genuine smile she'd managed since the evening began. "Detective Blackwood, I thought you'd never ask." She turned to Miss Cho. "I want to see your tea shop. And I want to see that saucer with the coded tea stains."

"It's nearly midnight," Blackwood protested.

"The dead don't keep regular hours, Detective. And neither, apparently, do killers." Lillian began gathering her examination tools. "Mrs. Ashworth was murdered for a reason. If we want to find her killer, we need to understand what she knew, and who was desperate enough to kill her for it."

Miss Cho nodded slowly. "Very well. But we must be careful. If someone was willing to commit murder in my establishment once…" She left the threat unfinished.

As the group prepared to leave, Edmund caught Lillian's arm. "My dear, perhaps you should let the detective handle this investigation. It could be dangerous."

Lillian patted her father's hand affectionately. "Don't worry, Father. I'll be careful."

"That's exactly what I'm afraid of," Edmund muttered, but he didn't try to stop her.

As they climbed the basement stairs, Lillian felt the familiar thrill of a hunt beginning. Mrs. Ashworth's secrets had died with her, but secrets had a way of leaving traces. And Lillian Cross had made a career of reading the stories that others preferred to leave buried.

The gaslight flickered as they emerged into the parlor, casting long shadows that seemed to dance with anticipation. Outside, the fog had thickened, muffling the sounds of the city and creating a world where anything might be possible, including murder disguised as natural death.

But Lillian had learned long ago that death was rarely natural when money and secrets were involved.

And in Manhattan's glittering society, both were always in abundant supply.

The fog transformed Manhattan into a ghost city. Gas lamps struggled to pierce the thick gray curtain that had descended from the harbor, their halos of light creating isolated islands of visibility in an ocean of shadow. Lillian pulled her wool cloak tighter as their small group navigated the cobblestone streets, their footsteps echoing hollowly in the muffled quiet.

"How much farther?" Detective Blackwood asked, his voice barely carrying through the mist.

"Two more blocks," Miss Cho replied, moving with the confidence of someone who knew these streets intimately. "The Celestial Garden is just ahead."

The tea shop materialized from the fog like something from a fairy tale, a narrow building squeezed between a haberdashery and a milliner's shop, its painted sign swaying gently in the damp air. Warm light glowed through frosted windows, and delicate wind chimes sang softly from the covered entrance.

Miss Cho produced a ring of keys and unlocked the front door. "Please, come in quickly."

The interior was a study in elegant contrasts. Dark wooden tables and chairs sat beneath paper lanterns that cast warm, golden light. Delicate porcelain covered the walls, cups, saucers, and serving pieces arranged in intricate patterns that seemed almost like writing. The air held the lingering fragrance of jasmine and bergamot, though underneath lay something else—the faint metallic scent of fear.

"Where did it happen?" Lillian asked.

Miss Cho gestured toward a corner table near the large front window. "There. Mrs. Ashworth always preferred that spot, she could see who was coming and going on the street."

Lillian approached the table, noting the careful way it had been cleaned. Too carefully. "You washed everything."

"The police released the scene after Dr. Morrison's examination. I had customers coming." Miss Cho stopped herself. "I saved what you needed to see."

She disappeared through a curtained doorway and returned carrying a porcelain tea service on a lacquered tray. Even in the lantern light, Lillian could see the dark stains on the saucer where tea had spilled during Mrs. Ashworth's collapse.

"May I?" Lillian held out her hands for the saucer.

Miss Cho hesitated. "Be very careful. The pattern is… significant."

Lillian held the saucer up to the light, studying the arrangement of tea stains. At first glance, they appeared random, the natural result of liquid spilling when a cup was dropped. But as she rotated the porcelain slowly, a pattern began to emerge.

"Detective, look at this." She angled the saucer so Blackwood could see. "These aren't random spills."

The stains formed a deliberate arrangement, three large drops in a triangular pattern, with smaller spots arranged around them like points of a compass. Between the larger stains, thin lines of tea had been deliberately drawn, creating what looked almost like a map.

"It's a code," Blackwood said, his earlier skepticism replaced by fascination.

"More than that," Miss Cho said quietly. "It's a message. Mrs. Ashworth was trying to tell us something before she died."

Lillian set the saucer on the table and pulled out her notebook, quickly sketching the pattern. "What does it mean?"

Miss Cho moved to the wall of porcelain, her fingers trailing along one of the display cases. "To understand that, you need to know about the real business conducted in establishments like this."

"Which is?" Blackwood prompted.

Instead of answering directly, Miss Cho selected a delicate teacup from the display and placed it on the table. The cup was beautiful, white porcelain decorated with a pattern of blue flowers and gold trim. But as Lillian looked closer, she realized the floral pattern wasn't merely decorative.

"The chrysanthemums represent patience," Miss Cho explained, pointing to the various flowers painted on the cup. "The peonies symbolize honor, the lotus indicates rebirth. To someone who knows how to read them, these patterns convey meaning beyond mere decoration."

"You're talking about a code," Lillian said. "A way to pass messages without speaking."

"Precisely. Manhattan society is full of people

who need to communicate... discreetly. Affairs of the heart, business arrangements that shouldn't be discussed in public, information that could be valuable to the right buyer." Miss Cho's smile held no warmth.
"Tea shops provide the perfect cover. Ladies meet for perfectly innocent social calls, and if messages happen to be exchanged through the arrangement of cups and saucers, well, who would suspect such a thing?"

Detective Blackwood was staring at the wall of porcelain with new understanding. "You're running a spy network."

"I'm running a business," Miss Cho corrected. "Information is a commodity, Detective. Like silk or silver, it has value to those who know how to use it."

Lillian returned her attention to the stained saucer, comparing it to her sketch. "So Mrs. Ashworth was trying to leave a message in the tea stains. But for whom?"

"For whoever found her body, I assume. She must have realized she was dying and used her final moments to point toward her killer."

"Or toward the reason she was killed," Blackwood added grimly.

Miss Cho nodded toward a cabinet behind the counter. "There's something else you should see."

She retrieved a leather-bound ledger and set it on the table, opening it to reveal pages covered with neat handwriting. Names, dates, and cryptic notations filled the columns.

"Mrs. Ashworth's account," Miss Cho explained. "She was one of my most... active clients."

Lillian scanned the entries, recognizing several prominent Manhattan family names. "She was buying information about all of these people?"

"And selling it. Mrs. Ashworth had a talent for discovering secrets and a gift for knowing exactly who would pay the most to learn them." Miss Cho's finger traced down the page. "Look at her last few transactions."

The final entries were dated within the past week. Three names appeared repeatedly: Penrose, Hartwell, and Blackwell.

"Penrose," Lillian murmured. "Where have I heard that name?"

"Alistair Penrose," Blackwood said. "That young journalist who's been stirring up trouble with his newspaper stories. Always sniffing around police investigations, looking for scandal."

"And Hartwell and Blackwell… those were the women with Mrs. Ashworth when she died," Lillian added.

Miss Cho closed the ledger carefully.

"According to my records, Mrs. Ashworth recently acquired information about all three of them. Expensive information."

"What sort of information?" Lillian asked.

"The sort that could destroy reputations, end marriages, or derail political careers." Miss Cho met Lillian's eyes. "The sort that people kill to protect."

Lillian studied the tea stain pattern again, a theory beginning to form. "Miss Cho, do you have other examples of this coded messaging? I want to understand how it works."

Miss Cho retrieved several more saucers from behind the counter, each bearing different arrangements of deliberate stains and marks. She explained the basic symbols, triangles for danger, circles for money, straight lines pointing to specific locations or people.

"This pattern," Lillian said, pointing to Mrs. Ashworth's saucer, "what does it tell us?"

Miss Cho studied it carefully. "The triangular arrangement suggests immediate danger. These smaller marks… they could be numbers, or perhaps initials. And this line pointing toward the door, that might indicate the source of the threat."

"Someone who was coming to the tea shop," Blackwood concluded. "Someone Mrs. Ashworth knew would be arriving."

"Which means her killer was either already here when she arrived, or she was expecting them," Lillian said. "This wasn't a random attack."

A sudden sound from the street made them all freeze, footsteps on the cobblestones, approaching the tea shop. Miss Cho quickly extinguished two of the lanterns, plunging the room into dimmer light.

"We should go," she whispered. "If someone sees lights in here at this hour, they'll ask questions."

But the footsteps had stopped directly outside the shop. Through the frosted window, they could see a dark figure standing motionless in the fog.

Detective Blackwood's hand moved instinctively to his coat, where Lillian assumed he kept a weapon. "Back door?" he whispered.

Miss Cho nodded toward the curtained doorway. "Through the kitchen."

As they gathered the evidence, the stained saucer, the ledger, Lillian's sketches, the figure outside began testing the door handle. The brass knob turned slowly, as if the person were checking whether it was locked.

"Now," Miss Cho breathed.

They slipped through the curtained doorway into a small kitchen that smelled of tea leaves and spices. Miss Cho led them to a narrow door that opened onto an alley behind the building. The fog was even thicker here, providing perfect cover as they emerged into the night. Behind them, they heard the faint sound of breaking glass.

"They're inside," Blackwood whispered.

"Who do you think it was?" Lillian asked as they hurried down the alley.

"Someone who knows Mrs. Ashworth visited the tea shop regularly," Miss Cho replied. "Someone looking for the same evidence we just found."

"Or someone making sure that evidence disappears," Blackwood added grimly.

They reached the street and paused in the shelter of a doorway. The fog swirled around them like a living thing, concealing secrets and revealing danger in equal measure.

"We need somewhere safe to examine what we've found," Lillian said. "Somewhere we won't be interrupted."

"My rooms are too public," Blackwood said "Too many people coming and going at the boarding house."

Miss Cho was quiet for a moment. "There's a place. Private, secure. But you'll have to trust me."

Lillian looked at the tea shop owner, this woman who ran coded spy networks behind the façade of serving afternoon tea, and made her decision. "Lead the way."

As they disappeared into the fog-shrouded streets, none of them noticed the figure that detached itself from the shadows near the tea shop's front door. The figure watched them go, then melted back into the mist like a ghost returning to its haunting grounds.

In the Celestial Garden, broken glass glittered on the floor like fallen stars, and the carefully arranged porcelain lay in pieces, another pattern destroyed, another message silenced.

But some secrets, once unleashed, refused to stay buried. And Mrs. Vivian Ashworth's final message was already beginning to speak to those who knew how to listen.

Miss Cho led them through a maze of narrow streets that Lillian had never seen despite living in Manhattan her entire life. These weren't the grand avenues of Fifth Avenue or even the familiar tenement blocks of the Lower East Side. This was the hidden city, a network of alleys and courtyards that existed in the spaces between the official map, where immigrants carved out lives in the shadows of respectability.

"Where exactly are we going?" Detective Blackwood asked for the third time, his Irish brogue thickening with suspicion.

"Patience, Detective," Miss Cho replied without slowing her pace. "Some secrets require proper introduction."

They turned down an alley so narrow that Lillian could touch both walls with her outstretched arms. The fog seemed thinner here, held back by the close-pressed buildings like water unable to flow uphill.

Gas lamps were scarce, leaving them to navigate by the faint glow of curtained windows and the occasional flash of a late streetcar's headlamp in the distance.

"Here," Miss Cho stopped before what appeared to be a solid brick wall. But as Lillian watched, the tea shop owner pressed a specific sequence of bricks, and a section of the wall swung inward on silent hinges. "Quickly."

They stepped through the hidden entrance into a warmly lit corridor lined with rich carpets and papered walls. The transformation was so sudden and complete that Lillian felt as though she'd walked through a portal into another world entirely.

"What is this place?" she whispered.

"The real Manhattan," Miss Cho replied, leading them down the corridor. "The one that exists behind the façade your newspapers and society columns pretend to show."

The corridor opened into a circular room that took Lillian's breath away. Books lined the walls from floor to ceiling, but these weren't the leather-bound classics one might find in a Fifth Avenue mansion's library. These were journals, ledgers, files bound in plain covers, the accumulated documentation of secrets. At the center of the room sat a massive mahogany table surrounded by comfortable chairs, and suspended above it hung an intricate chandelier that cast warm light over everything.

But it was the people in the room that truly surprised her.

"Miss Cross, Detective Blackwood," Miss Cho said formally, "welcome to the Repository."

A woman rose from one of the chairs, elderly but with the bearing of someone accustomed to command. Her silver hair was perfectly arranged despite the late hour, and her dark dress was cut from expensive fabric but designed for practicality rather than fashion.

When she spoke, her voice carried the authority of someone used to being obeyed.

"I am Mrs. Adelaide Whitmore," she said, extending a gloved hand to Lillian. "Evelina has told me about your… investigation."

"Mrs. Whitmore," Lillian said carefully, recognizing the name from the society pages. "The philanthropist."

"Among other things." Mrs. Whitmore's smile held secrets. "Please, sit. We have much to discuss."

As they settled around the table, Lillian counted five other people in the room, men and women of varying ages and social classes, united by an air of shared purpose. A young man with ink-stained fingers and the intense eyes of a born journalist. An older woman whose calloused hands suggested manual labor despite her neat appearance. A middle-aged man in expensive but understated clothing who kept checking a gold pocket watch.

"What exactly is this place?" Detective Blackwood asked, his hand still resting near his coat, near his weapon, Lillian realized.

"The Repository serves many functions," Mrs. Whitmore explained. "Library, meeting place, sanctuary for those who deal in Manhattan's most valuable commodity, information. We are what you might call a society of truth-seekers."

"Spies," Blackwood said bluntly.

"Investigators," Mrs. Whitmore corrected gently. "There's a difference, Detective. Spies serve governments or armies. We serve justice."

Miss Cho placed the stained saucer and Mrs. Ashworth's ledger on the table. "Vivian's final message. We need to decode it properly."

The group leaned forward with obvious interest. Mrs. Whitmore put on a pair of spectacles and studied the tea stain pattern carefully.

"Evelina, bring the cipher key," she said after a moment.

Miss Cho retrieved a leather portfolio from one of the bookshelves and spread several papers across the table. They were covered with symbols, patterns, and corresponding meanings, a complete guide to the coded messaging system Lillian had glimpsed at the tea shop.

"Mrs. Ashworth was one of our most... enthusiastic participants," Mrs. Whitmore explained as she compared the stained saucer to the cipher key. "She had a talent for uncovering secrets, though she wasn't always careful about how she used them."

"Meaning she sold information to the highest bidder rather than using it for justice," the young journalist said. His voice carried a note of disapproval.

"Not everyone shares our idealistic goals, Mr. Penrose," Mrs. Whitmore replied mildly.

Lillian looked up sharply. "Alistair Penrose? You're the journalist who's been writing those exposé pieces about corruption in the police department."

Penrose colored slightly. "Among other things. And you're the mortician's daughter who's been poking her nose into matters that don't concern her."

"Vivian's murder concerns all of us," Mrs. Whitmore said firmly before Lillian could respond. "Now, let's see what she was trying to tell us."

Using the cipher key, she began translating the pattern of tea stains. "The triangular arrangement indicates immediate danger—we already knew that. These smaller marks... they spell out a name."

"Whose name?" Detective Blackwood leaned forward.

Mrs. Whitmore's expression grew troubled. "Duval."

A collective intake of breath went around the table. Even Detective Blackwood seemed to recognize the significance.

"As in the Widow Duval?" Lillian asked. "The woman who funds half the reform movements in the city?"

"The very same," Mrs. Whitmore confirmed. "Mrs. Margaret Duval, one of Manhattan's most generous philanthropists, and one of our most important sponsors."

"Vivian was pointing to Mrs. Duval as her killer?" Miss Cho asked, disbelief evident in her voice.

"Or as the reason she was killed," Lillian said thoughtfully. She turned to Mrs. Whitmore. "What sort of information did Mrs. Ashworth have about Mrs. Duval?"

Mrs. Whitmore consulted the ledger, running her finger down the columns of entries. "According to this, Vivian recently discovered something about the source of Mrs. Duval's wealth. Something that contradicted the official story of her late husband's business success."

"What kind of contradiction?" Detective Blackwood asked.

"The kind that suggests Mr. Duval's fortune wasn't earned through legitimate business ventures," Penrose said grimly. "I've been investigating the Duval family finances for months. There are... irregularities."

Mrs. Whitmore closed the ledger with a snap. "Which brings us to the real question—was Vivian killed because of what she knew about Mrs. Duval, or was she killed by Mrs. Duval to protect those secrets?"

"There's a third possibility," Lillian said slowly. "Someone else knew what Mrs. Ashworth had discovered and killed her to prevent that information from reaching Mrs. Duval—or to frame Mrs. Duval for the murder."

The room fell silent as everyone considered this possibility.

"We need to speak with Mrs. Duval," Detective

Blackwood said finally.

"That won't be possible," Mrs. Whitmore replied. "Margaret left the city yesterday morning. Her housekeeper said she received an urgent telegram and departed for her estate in Newport immediately."

"How convenient," Penrose muttered.

"Or how suspicious," Lillian added. She stood and began pacing around the table, her mind working through the possibilities. "What if Mrs. Duval didn't flee because she was guilty? What if she left because she was afraid?"

"Afraid of whom?" Miss Cho asked.

"The same person who killed Mrs. Ashworth. Think about it, if Mrs. Ashworth had damaging information about Mrs. Duval, and if Mrs. Duval suspected someone was planning to use that information against her…"

"She might have left the city to protect herself," Detective Blackwood finished. "Which means the real killer is still here, probably planning their next move."

Mrs. Whitmore nodded approvingly. "Very good, Miss Cross. You think like one of us."

"One of you?"

"Someone who understands that in Manhattan society, the most dangerous person is rarely the one who commits the crime, it's the one who benefits from it."

A soft chime echoed through the room, and one of the other members—the man with the pocket watch, stood quickly.

"Someone's coming," he said quietly. "Multiple footsteps in the main alley."

Mrs. Whitmore was already moving toward a different exit. "Everyone out. Use the secondary routes."

"What about the evidence?" Lillian asked, reaching for the ledger.

"Leave it," Mrs. Whitmore commanded. "The Repository has survived this long by knowing when to retreat and when to fight. Tonight, we retreat."

As the group dispersed through various hidden passages, Lillian found herself following Miss Cho down a narrow staircase that led to what appeared to be a wine cellar. Detective Blackwood was close behind them, and she could hear his breathing, sharp with tension.

"How did they find us?" he whispered.

"The same way we found Mrs. Ashworth's body," Miss Cho replied grimly. "Someone's been watching, waiting for the right moment to strike."

They emerged through another concealed entrance into a different alley, this one emptying onto a main street where late streetcars still rattled past. The fog had begun to lift, revealing patches of star-filled sky between the tenement rooftops.

"Now what?" Lillian asked.

Miss Cho checked the street carefully before answering. "Now we assume that whoever killed Vivian knows we're investigating. Which means we're all in danger."

"All the more reason to solve this quickly," Detective Blackwood said. "Before they have a chance to silence anyone else."

Lillian pulled her cloak tighter against the cold air and looked back toward the hidden entrance they'd just used. Somewhere in the maze of Manhattan's secret passages, powerful people were playing a deadly game with information as their weapon and murder as their tool.

But she'd learned something important tonight. She wasn't alone in her desire for truth. The Repository and its members represented something she'd never imagined—a network of people committed to uncovering the secrets that Manhattan's elite preferred to keep buried.

“Detective,” she said as they walked toward the main street to find a cab. “Tomorrow, we’re going to Newport.”

“Are we now? And what makes you think Mrs. Duval will agree to see us?”

Lillian smiled, feeling the familiar thrill of a plan taking shape. “Because we’re going to tell her we have information about Mrs. Ashworth's murder. Information that could clear her name, or destroy her completely.”

“And do we?”

“Not yet,” Lillian admitted. “But we will by the time we reach Newport. After all, the best way to catch a killer is to make them think they've already won.”

As their cab rattled through the fog-shrouded streets toward home, none of them noticed the figure that emerged from the alley they’d just left. The figure watched their carriage disappear into the night, then turned and walked back toward the shadows, moving with the confidence of someone who knew exactly where their quarry was headed next.

The morning train to Newport cut through the Connecticut countryside like a steel arrow aimed at the heart of America's aristocracy. Lillian pressed her face to the window, watching autumn maples blur past in shades of gold and crimson. Beside her, Detective Blackwood sat rigidly upright, clearly uncomfortable in the borrowed gentleman's clothing that Miss Cho had somehow procured for their journey.

"Remind me again why I'm pretending to be your cousin?" he muttered, adjusting his starched collar with obvious distaste.

"Because Mrs. Duval won't receive a Lower East Side police detective," Lillian replied without taking her eyes from the window. "But she might see Miss Lillian Cross and her cousin, Mr. Nathan Blackwood, who are researching genealogical records for a book about prominent Manhattan families."

"And what happens when she realizes we're investigating her for murder?"

"Then we improvise." Lillian finally turned to look at him, noting how the fine clothes transformed his appearance. The rough edges were still there, the calloused hands, the watchful eyes of a man used to danger, but now he looked like a gentleman who'd earned his calluses through boxing or sailing rather than street fighting. "You clean up rather well, Detective."

Blackwood's cheeks colored slightly. "Miss Cho has expensive tastes in menswear."

"Miss Cho has many talents we're only beginning to discover." Lillian consulted the pocket watch her father had given her, a Christmas gift three years ago that she treasured for its precision. "We should arrive within the hour. Are you ready for this?"

"I've questioned murderers before, Miss Cross."

"But have you questioned them in their own ballrooms while pretending to be someone else entirely?" Lillian smiled at his expression. "Newport society operates by different rules than the tenements, Detective. Here, the deadliest weapons are raised eyebrows and whispered rumors."

The train began to slow as they approached Newport station, and Lillian felt the familiar flutter of anticipation that preceded a confrontation. She'd spent the early morning hours researching everything she could find about Margaret Duval—society pages, charity announcements, even her late husband's business records. The picture that emerged was of a woman who wielded influence like other people used money: carefully, strategically, and with devastating effect when necessary.

Newport in October was a study in faded grandeur. The massive "cottages" that lined the cliff walks stood like monuments to excess, their windows reflecting the gray Atlantic sky. Most were already shuttered for the season, their wealthy owners having retreated to warmer climates or urban mansions. But the Duval estate, perched on a promontory overlooking the sea, blazed with light despite the overcast day.

Their hired carriage wound up the circular drive, past gardens that were still meticulously maintained despite the approaching winter. Lillian counted at least six gardeners at work, their tools glinting in the pale sunlight. Either Mrs. Duval was expecting to remain in Newport for some time, or she was using activity to mask anxiety.

"Nervous?" Blackwood asked as they climbed the marble steps to the front door.

"Terrified," Lillian admitted. "Which means we're probably on the right track."

The butler who answered their knock was a study in professional discretion—tall, silver-haired, and possessed of the sort of face that revealed nothing while observing everything. His eyes catalogued their appearance, their posture, even the quality of their shoes before he spoke.

"Good afternoon. May I help you?"

"Miss Lillian Cross and Mr. Nathan Blackwood," Lillian said, producing a calling card that Miss Cho had somehow created overnight. "We're here to see Mrs. Duval regarding our research into prominent Manhattan families. I believe she's expecting us."

It was a calculated bluff, but the butler's expression didn't change. "Please wait in the morning room. I'll inform Mrs. Duval of your arrival."

They were shown into a room that exemplified Newport's unique brand of ostentation. French furniture competed with Italian marble, while paintings by European masters hung beside portraits of American robber barons. Through tall windows, they could see the Atlantic stretching to the horizon, its gray surface broken by whitecaps that matched the stormy sky.

"She's coming," Blackwood said quietly, his trained ear catching the sound of approaching footsteps.

Margaret Duval entered the room like a queen receiving supplicants. She was smaller than Lillian had expected, barely five feet tall, but she commanded attention through sheer force of personality. Her silver hair was arranged in a severe chignon, and her black mourning dress was cut from fabric that probably cost more than most people earned in a year. But it was her eyes that truly impressed, dark, intelligent, and missing nothing.

"Miss Cross, Mr. Blackwood," she said, her voice carrying the authority of someone accustomed to deference. "Please, be seated. I confess myself curious about this genealogical research you mentioned."

Lillian took the offered chair, noting how Mrs. Duval positioned herself with the light behind her, making her face difficult to read. "We're investigating the interconnected histories of Manhattan's prominent families, particularly their business relationships during the 1870s and early 1880s."

"Fascinating period," Mrs. Duval replied smoothly. "So much… opportunity for those with vision and courage."

"Indeed. We were particularly interested in your late husband's partnership with the Ashworth family. Such a successful collaboration, from what we've learned."

For just an instant, Mrs. Duval's composure flickered. It was barely perceptible, a slight tightening around her eyes, but Lillian caught it.

"The Ashworth family," Mrs. Duval repeated carefully. "I'm afraid that partnership ended many years ago. Before poor Vivian's recent… difficulty."

"You heard about Mrs. Ashworth's death?" Blackwood asked, leaning forward slightly.

"Such tragic news travels quickly, even to Newport." Mrs. Duval's smile didn't reach her eyes. "Heart failure, I believe? So sudden, so unexpected."

"Actually," Lillian said, watching Mrs. Duval's face carefully, "the police now believe she was murdered."

This time, the reaction was unmistakable. Mrs. Duval's teacup rattled against its saucer as her hand trembled slightly. She set it down quickly, but not before Lillian noticed the genuine shock in her expression.

"Murdered?" Mrs. Duval's voice was barely above a whisper. "But who would… why would anyone…"

"That's what we're trying to determine," Blackwood said gently. "Mrs. Ashworth had been collecting information about various prominent families. Information that someone apparently killed her to suppress."

Mrs. Duval stood abruptly and walked to the window, her back to them as she gazed out at the restless sea. When she spoke again, her voice was steady but strained.

"I received a telegram two days ago. Anonymous. It said that if I didn't leave Manhattan immediately, I would meet the same fate as Vivian Ashworth." She turned to face them, and Lillian saw fear in those intelligent eyes. "At the time, I thought it meant I would die of heart failure. Now…"

"Now you know it was a death threat," Lillian finished.

Mrs. Duval nodded. "I came here not because I was guilty of anything, but because I was terrified. Vivian's death wasn't natural, and whoever killed her wanted me to know I could be next."

"What information did Mrs. Ashworth have about you?" Blackwood asked.

Mrs. Duval returned to her chair, seeming to age a decade in the space of a few steps. "Something I thought was buried forever. Something about my husband's business dealings in the early days of our marriage."

She paused, clearly struggling with how much to reveal. "Mr. Duval's fortune wasn't entirely... legitimately acquired. At least not in the beginning. There were partnerships with men who weren't particular about the law, investments in enterprises that operated in the shadows of respectability."

"What sort of enterprises?" Lillian asked gently.

"Import businesses that brought in more than silk and spices. Construction companies that used materials of questionable origin. Financial institutions that asked few questions about the source of their deposits." Mrs. Duval's voice grew steadier as she spoke, as if confession were bringing relief. "Edmund, my husband, eventually extricated himself from those partnerships, but not before they'd made him very wealthy."

"And Mrs. Ashworth discovered this?"

"She'd been researching old shipping records, business licenses, partnership agreements. The sort of documents that most people assume are lost to time, but which can still be found if one knows where to look." Mrs. Duval smiled bitterly. "Vivian was very good at knowing where to look."

Blackwood leaned forward. "Was she blackmailing you?"

"Not yet. But she would have, eventually. Vivian had a talent for finding the exact price that would cause maximum discomfort without quite destroying her target." Mrs. Duval's expression hardened. "She was a parasite who fed on other people's shame."

"Strong words for someone who's supposedly innocent," Lillian observed.

"I despised Vivian Ashworth, Miss Cross. She represented everything that's wrong with Manhattan society—the casual cruelty, the willingness to destroy lives for profit, the corruption that masquerades as respectability." Mrs. Duval met Lillian's eyes steadily. "But I didn't kill her. I wouldn't have needed to."

"What do you mean?"

Mrs. Duval stood again and walked to an ornate desk near the window. She returned with a leather portfolio, which she placed on the table between them.

"I mean that Vivian wasn't the only one who knew how to research inconvenient truths. Over the past few months, I'd been conducting my own investigation into her activities." She opened the portfolio to reveal newspaper clippings, photographs, and handwritten notes. "I was prepared to destroy her reputation completely if she tried to blackmail me."

Lillian examined the contents of the portfolio. Photographs showed Mrs. Ashworth meeting with various unsavory characters in questionable locations. Newspaper clippings documented scandals that had been quietly covered up, but not before Mrs. Ashworth had profited from them. The handwritten notes detailed a pattern of blackmail, extortion, and betrayal that painted Mrs. Ashworth as far more than a simple gossip.

"She was working with criminals," Lillian realized, studying a photograph that showed Mrs. Ashworth exchanging money with a man whose face was obscured by shadow.

"Among others. Vivian had clients who weren't interested in society gossip, they wanted information they could use to commit crimes or avoid prosecution for crimes already committed." Mrs. Duval's voice carried cold satisfaction. "I was going to expose everything if she threatened me."

"But someone killed her first," Blackwood said thoughtfully.

"Someone who couldn't afford to have their secrets exposed, even if it meant destroying Vivian in the process." Mrs. Duval closed the portfolio. "Someone who had more to lose than I did."

Lillian felt pieces of the puzzle beginning to shift and align. "Mrs. Duval, who else knew you were investigating Mrs. Ashworth?"

"No one. I was very careful to—" She stopped, her face paling. "Oh God."

"What is it?"

"My secretary. Mr. Pemberton. He helped me organize the research, arrange for the photographs to be taken. He knew everything." Mrs. Duval's voice rose with panic. "If he told someone, if he sold that information…"

"Where is Mr. Pemberton now?" Blackwood asked urgently.

"In Manhattan. I left him there to handle my correspondence, manage my affairs." Mrs. Duval was already moving toward the door. "We have to warn him. If someone killed Vivian to prevent exposure, and if they know that I have evidence…"

"They'll kill him too," Lillian finished grimly.

As they prepared for the urgent journey back to Manhattan, Lillian realized that their investigation had taken a deadly turn. What had begun as a single murder was revealing itself to be part of something much larger and more dangerous. Someone in Manhattan's elite circles was willing to kill repeatedly to protect their secrets.

And unless they moved quickly, Mr. Pemberton would be the next to die.

The train back to the city couldn't move fast enough for any of them. Outside the windows, the autumn landscape flew past in a blur of dying colors, while inside their compartment, three unlikely allies planned their next move in a game where the stakes were measured in lives rather than money.

But in Manhattan, their enemies were already making moves of their own.

The hansom cab flew through the darkening streets of Manhattan as if the devil himself were giving chase. Lillian gripped the leather seat as they careened around a corner, the wheels skidding on cobblestones still slick from the morning's rain. Beside her, Detective Blackwood checked his service revolver for the third time since leaving Grand Central Station.

"The address again?" the detective called to Mrs. Duval, who sat opposite them with the rigid posture of someone barely containing panic.

"Gramercy Park, number thirty-seven. The brown stone with the green shutters." Her voice was steady, but her gloved hands trembled slightly. "Pemberton has rooms on the second floor."

They'd made the journey from Newport in record time, but Lillian feared it still wasn't fast enough. The afternoon train had seemed to crawl through

Connecticut while her mind raced through increasingly dire scenarios. If their deductions were correct, if someone had killed Mrs. Ashworth to prevent the exposure of criminal activities—then Mr. Pemberton represented an even greater threat. He possessed not only Mrs. Duval's counter-investigation materials but also the organizational skills to make sense of them.

"There," Mrs. Duval pointed ahead. "That's the building."

Even from a distance, Lillian could see that something was wrong. The front door stood slightly ajar, unusual for a respectable boarding house in broad daylight. More concerning were the lack of lights in any of the second-floor windows and the small crowd of neighbors gathered on the sidewalk, their faces drawn with the particular expression people wore when witnessing tragedy.

"Pay the driver and tell him to wait," Blackwood instructed as he leaped from the still-moving cab. "We may need to leave quickly."

They approached the crowd carefully, listening to the fragments of conversation that drifted on the cool evening air.

"… found him this morning…"

"… such a quiet gentleman, never any trouble…"

"… police said it looked like his heart gave out, poor man…"

Lillian's stomach dropped. They were too late.

Mrs. Duval pushed through the crowd with the authority of someone accustomed to deference. "Excuse me, I'm Mrs. Margaret Duval. Mr. Pemberton was in my employ. What has happened?"

A middle-aged woman in a flour-dusted apron turned to her with obvious relief at having someone official to address. "Oh, ma'am, such terrible news. Poor Mr. Pemberton was found dead in his rooms this morning. The doctor said it was his heart—apparently he'd been having troubles, though he never mentioned it to any of us."

"His heart," Mrs. Duval repeated flatly.

"Found him at his desk, ma'am. Looked peaceful, the landlord said. Like he just… stopped."

Blackwood stepped forward, producing his police credentials. "Detective Nathaniel Blackwood, Metropolitan Police. Who discovered the body?"

The woman's eyes widened slightly at the sight of his badge. "Mr. Kowalski, the landlord. He went up when Mr. Pemberton didn't come down for breakfast. Always punctual as clockwork, he was."

"And the doctor who examined him?"

"Dr. Morrison, sir. He's the one who signed the certificate."

Lillian and Blackwood exchanged meaningful glances. Dr. Morrison, the same physician who'd pronounced Mrs. Ashworth's death natural without proper examination.

"We'd like to see the rooms," Blackwood said firmly.

"Oh, but sir, they've been sealed by the police."

"I *am* the police." Blackwood's voice carried the weight of authority. "And this is part of an ongoing investigation."

The crowd parted as they approached the building, Mrs. Duval following close behind. The landlord, a stocky man with kind eyes and worried expression, met them at the front door.

"Mr. Kowalski?" Blackwood showed his credentials again. "We need to examine Mr. Pemberton's rooms."

"Certainly, Detective. Though I'm not sure what you'll find. Poor man died natural as rain, according to Dr. Morrison." He led them up a narrow staircase to the second floor. "Never seen him sick a day in his life, mind you, but the heart's a mysterious thing."

Pemberton's rooms were modest but comfortable, a sitting area with a desk by the window, a small bedroom visible through an open doorway, and shelves lined with books and papers. At first glance, everything appeared normal. Too normal.

"Detective," Lillian said quietly, pointing to the desk. "Look at this."

The desktop was meticulously organized, pens in their holder, papers in neat stacks, an appointment calendar open to the current week. But there were telltale signs of disturbance for those who knew how to look. A slight indentation in the leather desk pad where something heavy had been removed. A pen lying at a slightly different angle than the others. Most tellingly, a thin layer of dust on the windowsill had been disturbed, as if someone had searched behind the curtains.

"Someone's been here," Blackwood observed, his voice low enough not to carry to the landlord, who was lingering nervously in the doorway.

Mrs. Duval moved to a filing cabinet in the corner. "Pemberton kept all my research materials in here." She tried the top drawer and found it locked. "The key should be…" She felt under the desk's middle drawer, then behind the calendar on the wall. "It's gone."

"Mr. Kowalski," Blackwood called. "Did anyone else have access to these rooms after Mr. Pemberton's body was discovered?"

The landlord stepped further into the room. "Well, Dr. Morrison examined him, of course. And there was a gentleman from his employer—said he needed to collect some business papers before they got mixed up with the personal effects."

"What did this gentleman look like?"

"Middle-aged, well-dressed. Had proper identification and everything. Said he was Mrs. Duval's business manager." Kowalski glanced at Mrs. Duval. "Seemed to know all about Mr. Pemberton's work."

"I don't have a business manager," Mrs. Duval said flatly. "What did he take?"

"Just some files from that cabinet there. Said they contained sensitive financial information that needed to be secured." The landlord's expression grew worried. "Was there something wrong with that?"

Before anyone could answer, Lillian heard footsteps on the stairs, multiple sets, moving with purpose. She caught Blackwood's eye and nodded toward the window.

"Mr. Kowalski," she said pleasantly, "perhaps you could show us Mr. Pemberton's bedroom? I'd like to see where he was found."

As the landlord moved toward the bedroom, Lillian quickly examined the window. It opened onto a fire escape that connected to the building's rear alley. She turned to find Blackwood and Mrs. Duval watching her with understanding.

The footsteps in the hallway paused outside the door.

"Detective Blackwood?" a voice called. "This is Captain Morrison, Metropolitan Police. We need to speak with you."

Blackwood's jaw tightened. Captain Morrison was his superior, the man who'd been increasingly critical of his investigations and increasingly friendly with Manhattan's wealthy elite.

"The window," Lillian whispered.

"We can't all fit…" Mrs. Duval began.

"You can." Blackwood drew his revolver and moved toward the door. "I'll handle Morrison."

"Don't be foolish," Lillian hissed. "If Morrison's involved in this, you'll be next."

The door handle began to turn.

Blackwood looked at Lillian with an expression

that held regret, determination, and something else she couldn't quite identify. "Get her to safety. Find the truth." He glanced toward Mrs. Duval. "And don't trust anyone in an official position until this is over."

"Detective Blackwood, open this door immediately," Captain Morrison's voice was sharp with authority.

Lillian grabbed Mrs. Duval's arm and pulled her toward the window. "Now."

They climbed through onto the fire escape just as the door to Pemberton's rooms burst open. Through the glass, Lillian could see Blackwood facing three men, Captain Morrison and two others she didn't recognize.

"Where are they, Blackwood?" Morrison's voice carried clearly through the window.

"Where are who, Captain?"

The sound of a fist connecting with flesh made Lillian flinch. Mrs. Duval gasped and started to move back toward the window, but Lillian held her firmly.

"We can't help him if we're captured too," she whispered.

They climbed down the fire escape as quietly as possible, but just as they reached the second-floor landing, one of the men inside spotted them through the window.

"There! On the fire escape!"

"Move," Lillian urged, and they clattered down the remaining flights as shouts erupted from the building.

They reached the alley and ran toward the street, where their cab still waited. But as they rounded the corner, Lillian saw two more men approaching from the opposite direction, clearly part of the same group.

"This way," Mrs. Duval said, pulling Lillian toward a narrow passage between buildings.

They found themselves in a maze of service alleys and courtyards that Mrs. Duval navigated with surprising confidence. Only when they were several blocks away, hidden in the doorway of a closed bakery, did they stop to catch their breath.

"How did you know about those passages?" Lillian gasped.

"My husband's business required… discretion. I learned the hidden routes of Manhattan out of necessity." Mrs. Duval's face was pale but determined. "The question now is where we go for help. If Captain Morrison is involved, we can't trust the police."

Lillian thought of the Repository, of Mrs. Whitmore and her network of information gatherers. But their last visit had ended in flight, and she wasn't sure the secret meeting place would still be secure.

"There's somewhere," she said finally. "But first, I need to retrieve something."

"What?"

"My father's embalming supplies." Lillian's mind was racing, forming a plan that was equal parts desperate and brilliant. "If Dr. Morrison has been signing false death certificates, covering up murders by claiming natural causes, there's only one way to prove it."

"Which is?"

Lillian met Mrs. Duval's eyes with grim determination. "We're going to examine Mr. Pemberton's body ourselves. And this time, we're going to do it properly."

As they made their way through the darkening streets toward Cross & Sons Funeral Parlor, neither woman noticed the figure that detached itself from the shadows behind them. Their pursuers had lost them for now, but in Manhattan's interconnected web of secrets and lies, there were always more hunters ready to take up the chase.

The game had become deadly serious, and the next move would determine whether they lived to expose the truth, or joined Mrs. Ashworth and Mr. Pemberton in their permanent silence.

The Cross & Sons Funeral Parlor stood dark and silent against the October night, its familiar brick facade offering the promise of sanctuary, or at least temporary refuge. Lillian used her key to open the rear entrance, leading Mrs. Duval through the narrow hallway past her father's office and into the preparation room where everything had begun three days ago.

"Where is your father?" Mrs. Duval asked, glancing around the basement chamber with obvious unease.

"Making arrangements with the Henley family." Lillian lit the oil lamps with practiced efficiency, casting warm light across the marble preparation tables. "A blessing, actually. He wouldn't approve of what we're about to do."

She moved to a locked cabinet and retrieved her examination tools, then paused at a second cabinet that held her father's more... specialized equipment. The embalming supplies, preservation chemicals, and most importantly, the substances used to detect various toxins in human tissue.

"Mrs. Duval, I need you to understand what we're undertaking," Lillian said, arranging her instruments on a clean cloth. "If we're caught performing an unauthorized examination, we'll be arrested. If we're caught by the people who killed Mr. Pemberton, we'll likely join him in the morgue."

Mrs. Duval had moved to the window, peering through the narrow glass at the alley beyond.

"And if we don't find proof that Dr. Morrison has been covering up murders, Detective Blackwood will disappear, and we'll never be safe again."

She turned back to Lillian with steel in her voice. "How do we get Mr. Pemberton's body?"

"That's the relatively easy part."

Lillian pulled out a city directory and flipped to the listings for morgues and coroners.

"Bodies awaiting burial are held at the municipal morgue until the family makes arrangements. Since Mr. Pemberton had no family in the city, he'll be in the unclaimed section."

"And we simply walk in and request to examine him?"

"We walk in, and I present myself as the mortician preparing him for burial on behalf of a distant relative who's wired funds."

Lillian had already begun forging the necessary paperwork, her pen moving quickly across official-looking letterhead she'd borrowed from her father's files.

"The night attendant knows me, we've done business before when families needed expedited services."

Mrs. Duval watched her work with admiration.

"You're quite accomplished at deception, Miss Cross."

"I prefer to think of it as creative problem-solving." Lillian finished the forged authorization and blotted the ink carefully. "The question is whether you're prepared for what we might find. Examining a body isn't like viewing someone in their coffin. It's… clinical. Often disturbing."

"I've seen death before, Miss Cross. My husband's passing wasn't peaceful." Mrs. Duval's voice carried old pain. "If Mr. Pemberton was murdered, I need to know. He died because of information he gathered for me."

They made their way through the darkened streets toward the municipal morgue, a grim stone building near the docks that processed the city's unclaimed dead. The night air carried the scent of rain and the distant smell of the harbor, salt, fish, and the indefinable odor of a working waterfront.

"Miss Cross?" Mrs. Duval spoke quietly as they walked. "What will you do if we prove that Dr. Morrison has been covering up murders?"

"Expose him. Along with whoever's been paying him to do it." Lillian adjusted her medical bag, feeling the weight of her instruments inside.

"The Repository has connections to honest journalists. If we can document the evidence properly…"

"And Detective Blackwood?"

Lillian's jaw tightened. "We'll find him. But first, we need proof that will force the honest police to act, regardless of Captain Morrison's involvement."

The municipal morgue was a study in institutional grimness, bare stone walls, harsh gas lighting, and the ever-present smell of carbolic acid that couldn't quite mask the odor of death. The night attendant, a thin man with prematurely gray hair, looked up from his newspaper as they entered.

"Miss Cross!" His face brightened with recognition. "Bit late for a pickup, isn't it?"

"Emergency request, Tommy. Family just wired funds from Boston for a Mr. Pemberton. He died yesterday, natural causes." She handed him the forged authorization. "They want the body prepared tonight for transport on the morning train."

Tommy examined the paperwork with the casual attention of someone who'd processed hundreds of similar requests.

"Pemberton… yeah, he's in the back. Poor fellow, dropped dead at his desk. Doctor said it was his heart."

"Dr. Morrison?" Lillian asked casually.

"That's the one. Quick examination, signed the certificate, done and dusted."

Tommy led them toward the storage area where bodies awaited processing. "Always efficient, Dr. Morrison is."

"Always," Lillian agreed, exchanging a meaningful glance with Mrs. Duval.

The storage area was lined with wooden tables, each bearing a sheet-covered form. Tommy consulted his ledger and led them to a table in the far corner.

"Here we are. Mr. Pemberton, age forty-two, heart failure."

He pulled back the sheet, revealing a middle-aged man with thinning brown hair and the pale, waxy complexion of recent death.

"Peaceful-looking, isn't he? Like he just went to sleep."

Too peaceful, Lillian thought. She'd seen enough natural deaths to recognize the subtle signs of distress that usually accompanied heart failure. Mr. Pemberton looked exactly like Mrs. Ashworth had, serene in a way that suggested his death had been quick and, from his perspective, unexpected.

"We'll need some privacy for the preparation," Lillian said. "Family's particular about the religious requirements."

"Of course, of course. I'll be in the front office if you need anything." Tommy retreated, leaving them alone with the body.

Lillian immediately began her examination, starting with the external signs she'd learned to read like text on a page. Mrs. Duval watched intently, her earlier squeamishness replaced by grim determination.

"No obvious trauma," Lillian murmured, running her magnifying glass over Mr. Pemberton's neck and arms. "But look here…" She indicated a tiny mark behind his left ear, nearly identical to the one she'd found on Mrs. Ashworth. "Injection site."

She scraped a sample from around the wound, then moved to examine his fingernails, gums, and eyes. Each discovery painted a clearer picture of what had actually happened.

"Dilated pupils, slight blue tinge to the fingernails, and this residue under his nails suggests he briefly struggled before losing consciousness." Lillian prepared a slide for microscopic examination. "Mrs. Duval, hold this lamp steady."

Under the microscope, the scraped sample revealed the same crystalline residue she'd found on Mrs. Ashworth, the telltale signature of an alkaloid poison. "Strychnine again," she confirmed. "Same method, same poison. This is definitely the work of the same killer."

"But who has access to medical-grade poisons and the knowledge to use them?" Mrs. Duval asked.

"A physician. Or someone with medical training." Lillian began documenting her findings, sketching and taking notes with the thoroughness of someone who knew this evidence might be their only chance for justice. "The question is whether Dr.

Morrison is the killer or just the one covering up the crimes."

A sound from the front office—voices, multiple sets of footsteps, made them both freeze.

"… should be in the back storage area…"

"… make it look like an accident, just like the others…"

"… Dr. Morrison wants this cleaned up tonight…"

Lillian grabbed Mrs. Duval's arm and pointed toward a service door at the rear of the storage room. They gathered their evidence quickly, but as they reached the door, they heard Tommy's voice, higher and more nervous than before.

"I don't know anything about unauthorized examinations. Miss Cross had proper paperwork…"

"Miss Cross isn't supposed to be here, you fool. She's interfering in official business."

The voice belonged to Captain Morrison, and it carried the cold authority of someone accustomed to having his orders followed without question.

The service door was locked. Lillian fumbled with her lock picks, a skill she'd acquired during a misspent adolescence, while Mrs. Duval kept watch.

"They're coming this way," Mrs. Duval whispered.

The lock clicked open just as the storage room door burst open behind them. They slipped through the service entrance into an alley that ran behind the morgue, but they could already hear pursuit beginning.

"This way," Mrs. Duval said, once again demonstrating her knowledge of Manhattan's hidden passages.

They ran through a maze of service alleys and side streets, but this time their pursuers were more organized. Lillian could hear coordinated shouts from multiple directions, they were being herded.

"The Repository," she gasped as they paused in the shadow of a loading dock. "Can you find it again?"

"Not from here. And we don't know if it's safe." Mrs. Duval was breathing hard, her elegant composure finally cracking under the strain.

"Where else can we go?" Lillian thought quickly. They needed somewhere unexpected, somewhere their enemies wouldn't think to look. Somewhere with resources they could use to get their evidence to the right people.

"The newspaper," she said suddenly. "Not the respectable papers—they're all in someone's pocket. But there's a small publication that's been covering police corruption. If we can get our evidence to them…"

"Which newspaper?"

"The Manhattan Observer. Alistair Penrose writes for them." Lillian felt a surge of hope.

"He's one of Mrs. Whitmore's people. If we can reach him…"

They set off through the darkened streets toward the newspaper district, carrying with them the evidence that could expose a conspiracy of murder and corruption reaching into the highest levels of Manhattan society. But behind them, their hunters were closing in, and dawn was still hours away.

The truth they carried was explosive enough to topple careers and destroy fortunes. The question was whether they would live long enough to reveal it.

In the distance, church bells began to toll midnight, marking not just the end of another day, but potentially the end of their desperate flight from those who killed to keep secrets buried.

The Manhattan Observer occupied a narrow building wedged between a haberdashery and a bakery, its modest facade giving no hint of the explosive stories that originated within its walls. Gas lights burned in the upper floors despite the late hour, testimony to the dedication of journalists who understood that corruption never slept, and neither could those who fought it.

Lillian pressed herself against the brick wall beside the building's entrance, catching her breath while scanning the street for signs of pursuit. Mrs. Duval stood beside her, no longer the elegant society matron who'd received them in Newport, but a woman transformed by desperation and determination.

"Are you certain Penrose will be here at this hour?" Mrs. Duval whispered.

"He lives above the office. And if I know

anything about journalists, he'll be awake." Lillian studied the building's facade, noting the fire escape that zigzagged up the side. "The question is whether our enemies have had the same idea."

As if summoned by her words, two figures emerged from the alley across the street. Even in the dim gaslight, Lillian recognized the purposeful movements of professional hunters. Captain Morrison's men had indeed anticipated their destination.

"Back door," Mrs. Duval murmured, pointing toward the narrow passage that ran between the Observer building and the bakery.

They slipped into the passage just as the two men began crossing the street. The rear of the building was a maze of fire escapes, service entrances, and the detritus of urban life. Lillian tried the back door and found it locked, but the fire escape ladder was within reach.

"Can you climb in that dress?" she asked.

Mrs. Duval glanced down at her elegant but impractical attire. "I suppose we'll find out."

They ascended as quietly as possible, the metal rungs cold beneath their hands and the October wind cutting through their clothes. Through the windows, Lillian could see the Observer's modest offices, desks covered with papers, manual typesetting equipment, and the organized chaos that characterized working newsrooms.

On the third floor, she spotted what she was looking for: a young man bent over a desk, his shirt sleeves rolled up and his hair disheveled from running his hands through it. Even through the glass, she could see the intensity that marked him as someone chasing a story.

She tapped lightly on the window.

Alistair Penrose looked up with the startled expression of someone accustomed to working alone at strange hours. When he saw two women on his fire escape, his first instinct appeared to be panic, but then recognition dawned.

"Miss Cross?" He hurried to open the window. "What in God's name are you doing out there?"

"Trying not to be murdered," Lillian replied, climbing through the window with as much dignity as she could manage. "Mr. Penrose, we need your help."

Mrs. Duval followed, her silk dress catching on the window frame in a way that would have horrified her under normal circumstances. "Mr. Penrose, I'm Margaret Duval. I believe Mrs. Whitmore mentioned my case?"

Penrose's expression sharpened immediately.

"The Ashworth murder? We thought you'd fled the city."

"I did. But the conspiracy followed me to Newport and nearly killed my secretary." Mrs. Duval moved away from the window, allowing Lillian to close it behind them.

"We have evidence. Proof that Dr. Morrison has been covering up murders by claiming they were natural deaths." Lillian said.

"What sort of evidence?"

Lillian opened her medical bag and spread their findings on Penrose's desk. "Forensic analysis of both victims showing identical injection sites and poison residue. Documented patterns proving the same killer used the same method. And witness testimony about Dr. Morrison's suspicious behavior."

Penrose examined the materials with the hungry expression of a journalist who'd stumbled onto the story of a lifetime.

"This is extraordinary work, Miss Cross. Where did you learn forensic techniques this advanced?"

"Necessity and curiosity. The question is whether you can get this published before they silence us permanently."

"They?"

Mrs. Duval took over the explanation, describing the conspiracy that reached from corrupt physicians to police captains, from blackmail schemes to systematic murder. As she spoke, Penrose's expression grew increasingly grim.

"If half of what you're saying is true, this reaches much higher than Dr. Morrison and Captain Morrison," he said finally. "Someone with significant resources and influence has been orchestrating this."

"Someone who could afford to pay for professional killings and official cover-ups," Lillian agreed. "Someone who had access to Mrs. Ashworth's blackmail materials and decided the risk was too great to tolerate."

A sound from the street below made them all freeze, carriages stopping, multiple sets of footsteps, voices giving quiet orders. Penrose moved to the window and peered down carefully.

"Four men, maybe more. They're surrounding the building."

"How long do we have?" Mrs. Duval asked.

"Minutes, if that." Penrose was already moving, gathering papers from his desk and stuffing them into a leather satchel. "But there's something you need to know. I've been investigating this story from another angle." He pulled out a folder marked with Mrs. Ashworth's name. "Vivian wasn't just collecting secrets randomly. She was working for someone—someone who wanted specific information about specific people."

"Who?" Lillian asked.

"That's what I've been trying to determine. But look at this." He spread several documents on the desk. "Every person she investigated, every secret she uncovered, they all connect to a single business venture from fifteen years ago."

Lillian studied the papers, seeing a pattern emerge. "The Hudson Valley Railway expansion. All these people were investors or contractors connected to that project."

"Exactly. And that project was plagued by scandals, safety violations that led to deaths, financial irregularities, environmental damage that was covered up." Penrose's voice grew excited despite their desperate circumstances. "Someone's been systematically eliminating everyone who could testify about what really happened."

"But why now? Why after fifteen years?"

Mrs. Duval had gone pale. "Because there's going to be an investigation. The federal government is finally looking into railway corruption from that era. If the truth about Hudson Valley came out…"

"It would destroy everyone involved," Penrose finished. "Not just financially, but criminally. We're talking about charges of manslaughter, fraud, bribery…" The sound of footsteps on the building's internal stairs cut him off. Their pursuers had found a way inside.

"Is there another way out?" Lillian asked.

Penrose nodded toward a door at the back of the office. "Roof access. But they'll expect that."

"Then we don't all go the same way." Lillian made a quick decision. "Mr. Penrose, you take the evidence and get it to someone who can publish it immediately. Mrs. Duval and I will create a distraction."

"I can't leave you—"

"You can and you will. This story is bigger than our individual survival." Lillian pressed her forensic notes into his hands. "Make sure the truth gets out."

The footsteps were getting closer, echoing up the narrow stairwell. Mrs. Duval moved to the fire escape window, but Lillian caught her arm.

"Not that way. They'll expect it." She pointed toward the front of the building. "The main stairs. Sometimes the most obvious escape is the one they least expect."

Penrose was already heading for the roof access. "There's a press conference tomorrow morning at City Hall, Mayor Whitman announcing the federal railway investigation. If I can get this evidence to the federal investigators…"

"Go," Lillian urged.

As Penrose disappeared through the roof access door, Lillian and Mrs. Duval moved toward the main stairwell. The building had gone eerily quiet, as if everyone involved were holding their breath.

"Miss Cross," Mrs. Duval whispered as they paused at the top of the stairs. "If we don't survive this, I want you to know that working with you has been the most honest thing I've done in years."

"We're going to survive," Lillian replied with more confidence than she felt. "And we're going to see justice done."

They began descending the stairs, moving as quietly as possible. Below them, Lillian could hear voices—at least three men coordinating their search. The ground floor would be heavily guarded, but there might be a window of opportunity if they moved quickly enough.

At the second-floor landing, she heard something that made her blood run cold: Detective Blackwood's voice, strained and clearly under duress.

"I told you, I don't know where they went. They could be anywhere in the city by now."

"Detective Blackwood is many things," came Captain Morrison's cold reply, "but he's not a good liar. You've been helping them from the beginning."

Lillian exchanged a glance with Mrs. Duval. Blackwood was alive, but clearly a prisoner. And from the sound of things, he was being used as bait.

The trap was closing around them, but at least now she knew where all the players were. The question was whether they could turn the hunters into the hunted before it was too late.

Dawn was still hours away, but Lillian could feel the approaching end of their desperate flight. One way or another, the truth about Mrs. Ashworth's murder, and the conspiracy behind it, would be revealed before the sun rose over Manhattan.

The only question was who would be alive to see it.

Lillian's mind raced through the building's layout, cataloguing every advantage they might possess. The Observer's cramped quarters, which had seemed like a disadvantage moments before, now offered possibilities. Narrow hallways meant their pursuers couldn't surround them easily. Multiple floors provided vertical escape routes. And most importantly, she was beginning to understand that their enemies' confidence might be their weakness.

"They expect us to run," she whispered to Mrs. Duval as they crept down the second-floor hallway. "Cornered prey fleeing in panic. What if we don't?"

"What do you have in mind?"

Lillian paused at a supply closet, testing the handle. Locked, but her lock picks made quick work of it. Inside, she found exactly what she'd hoped for—cleaning supplies, including several bottles of chemicals that would serve their purposes perfectly.

"Mrs. Duval, how much do you remember

about your husband's business associates? The ones who weren't entirely… legitimate?"

Mrs. Duval's eyes sharpened with understanding. "Enough to know that cornered criminals are most dangerous when they think they're safe."

From below came the sound of Morrison's voice, still questioning Blackwood. But there was something different now, a note of impatience that suggested the Captain was growing frustrated with his lack of progress.

"Search the upper floors," Morrison commanded. "They're here somewhere. And when you find them, remember, accidents happen to people who ask too many questions."

Heavy footsteps began ascending the stairs. At least two men, moving with the systematic efficiency of a military operation.

Lillian grabbed a bottle of ammonia and another of chlorine bleach, separately harmless cleaning supplies that became something entirely different when combined. "Can you create a distraction? Something that draws them toward the front of the building?"

Mrs. Duval nodded, moving toward a window that faced the street. She picked up a heavy glass paperweight from a nearby desk and weighed it in her hand. "On your signal."

The footsteps reached the second floor. Lillian could hear them separating, one moving toward the back offices, the other checking rooms systematically. They had perhaps thirty seconds before discovery.

She positioned herself near the stairwell, the chemical bottles ready in her hands. The mixture would create a choking cloud that would disable rather than kill, but more importantly, it would create chaos in the narrow confines of the stairway.

"Now," she whispered.

Mrs. Duval hurled the paperweight through the

front window. Glass exploded outward in a shower of glittering fragments, and the crash echoed through the building like a gunshot.

"Front window!" one of the men shouted. "They're trying to escape!"

Both sets of footsteps converged on the front of the building, exactly as Lillian had hoped. She moved quickly down the stairs, Mrs. Duval close behind her. The first floor was laid out as she'd expected from her glimpse through the windows, a main office area with desks and equipment, and smaller rooms branching off it.

She could see them now: Captain Morrison standing over Detective Blackwood, who was tied to a chair with obvious signs of rough treatment. Two other men were moving toward the front window, investigating the broken glass. A fourth man stood guard near what appeared to be the building's main entrance.

But it was the fifth figure that made Lillian's breath catch in her throat. Dr. Morrison stood in the shadows near the back of the room, a medical bag at his feet and a syringe in his hand. The family resemblance to Captain Morrison was unmistakable now that she saw them together, the same cold eyes, the same calculating expression.

Brothers, she realized. The conspiracy wasn't just professional, it was personal.

"See anything?" Captain Morrison called to his men at the window.

"Just broken glass. Could have been a diversion."

"Could have been," the Captain agreed, his voice carrying a note of suspicion. "Check the upper floors again. More carefully this time."

This was the moment. As the two men turned away from the window, Lillian stepped into the main office area, the chemical bottles already mixing in her hands.

"Gentlemen," she said pleasantly, as if she'd just arrived for afternoon tea. "I believe you've been looking for us."

The reaction was instantaneous. Captain Morrison spun toward her voice while his men scrambled for their weapons. But Lillian had already released the chemical mixture, and the narrow office space filled rapidly with a choking cloud of chloramine gas.

Shouting erupted as the men stumbled blindly through the toxic fog. Mrs. Duval appeared from the other direction, moving toward Detective Blackwood with a letter opener she'd found somewhere. The gas didn't affect her as severely, she was further from the source and had the advantage of expecting it.

"Get away from him!" Dr. Morrison's voice cut through the chaos. Unlike his associates, he'd recognized the chemical attack and had the presence of mind to cover his mouth and nose with his sleeve. The syringe was still in his other hand, and his intention was clear.

"Stop right there, or Detective Blackwood receives a lethal injection of strychnine."

Lillian froze. The gas was beginning to dissipate, but the confusion it had created gave her a few precious seconds to assess the situation. Captain Morrison was on his knees, coughing violently. Two of his men were stumbling toward the exits, temporarily blinded and incapacitated. The fourth was trying to draw his weapon while fighting the effects of the gas.

But Dr. Morrison stood clear of the worst effects, the syringe poised over Blackwood's neck.

"You've caused quite a lot of trouble, Miss Cross," the doctor said, his voice steady despite the chaos around him. "But it ends here."

"Does it?" Lillian asked, pulling a second set of bottles from her coat. "Because I have more chemicals, and you're standing much closer to Detective Blackwood than you were a moment ago. One wrong move, and you'll breathe as much of this as he will."

It was a bluff, she'd used her entire supply in the first attack. But Dr. Morrison didn't know that, and uncertainty flickered across his face.

"You're not a killer, Miss Cross. You're a mortician's daughter who's gotten in over her head."

"You're right," Lillian agreed. "I'm not a killer. But I am someone who's seen what your strychnine does to the human body. I've examined your victims, Doctor. I know exactly how they died."

She took a step closer, noting how his hand trembled slightly. "Mrs. Ashworth convulsed for nearly two minutes before the poison stopped her heart. Mr. Pemberton had enough time to realize what was happening, there were defensive wounds under his fingernails where he tried to fight you off."

Another step. The gas had cleared enough that she could see Blackwood's face. He was conscious, though blood trickled from a cut on his forehead, and his eyes were alert. He'd heard everything she'd said about the poison.

"You want to know what I think, Doctor?" Lillian continued, her voice conversational despite the syringe pointed at Blackwood's throat. "I think you've never actually watched someone die from strychnine poisoning. You inject them and leave, letting someone else find the bodies. You're a coward who kills from a distance."

"Shut up." Dr. Morrison's composure was cracking. Behind him, Captain Morrison was struggling to his feet, his face red from coughing.

"The Hudson Valley Railway," Lillian said, naming their deepest secret. "Fifteen years ago, you and your brother covered up dozens of deaths. Workers who died because safety equipment was too expensive. Families who were poisoned by contaminated water because environmental protection cut into profits."

"You don't know anything about—"

"I know everything." Mrs. Duval's voice came from behind him, calm and deadly. "I know about the federal investigation that's about to expose all of it. I know about the evidence that's already in the hands of honest journalists. And I know that killing us won't stop the truth from coming out."

Dr. Morrison spun toward her, but the movement brought him within Lillian's reach. She lunged forward, not for the syringe, but for his wrist, applying pressure to the nerve cluster that would force his hand to open.

The syringe clattered to the floor as Dr. Morrison cried out in pain. Blackwood, despite being tied to the chair, managed to kick backward, sending his captor stumbling into a desk.

"The weapon!" Mrs. Duval shouted, pointing to one of the incapacitated men's pistols that had fallen during the chaos.

But Captain Morrison was recovering faster than expected. He lurched toward the fallen weapon, his movements still unsteady but determined. Lillian realized with cold clarity that they were about to go from hunters back to hunted.

That was when the front door burst open, and federal agents flooded into the building.

"United States Marshals! Everyone on the ground, now!"

The voice carried absolute authority, and Lillian felt a surge of hope so powerful it nearly buckled her knees. Behind the Marshals, she could see a familiar figure—Alistair Penrose, his clothes disheveled and his face grim with determination.

"The evidence," he called to her across the chaos. "I got it to the federal investigators. They've been building a case for months… they just needed proof of the cover-up."

As the Marshals took control of the scene, securing weapons and detaining Morrison and his associates, Lillian finally allowed herself to breathe. But even as relief washed over her, she realized their ordeal was far from over.

Someone had been orchestrating this entire conspiracy, someone with the resources and connections to corrupt police captains and physicians. The Morrison brothers were just the instruments of a much larger criminal enterprise.

The real mastermind behind the Hudson Valley murders was still free, still dangerous, and now more desperate than ever.

The federal courthouse buzzed with activity as dawn broke over Manhattan. Marshal Benjamin Hayes, a weathered man with intelligent gray eyes, had commandeered a conference room where the key players in the Hudson Valley conspiracy sat around a mahogany table that had witnessed countless revelations over the years.

Lillian flexed her fingers, still sore from the previous night's confrontation. Beside her, Detective Blackwood nursed a cup of coffee and what would certainly become an impressive black eye. Mrs. Duval sat with the poise of someone who'd survived far worse than a night of running through Manhattan's shadows. Alistair Penrose scribbled notes with the fevered intensity of a journalist documenting history.

"The Morrison brothers have been quite

talkative since their arrest," Marshal Hayes began, consulting a thick file. "Especially once they realized they were facing federal charges for conspiracy to commit murder, obstruction of justice, and accessory to the original Hudson Valley crimes."

"What did they tell you?" Lillian asked.

"Enough to confirm what you suspected. They've been eliminating witnesses to the Hudson Valley Railway scandal for the past six months, ever since word leaked about the federal investigation." Hayes pulled out a photograph and placed it on the table. "But they didn't act alone, and they didn't identify the targets themselves."

The photograph showed a familiar figure standing beside a group of well-dressed men and women at what appeared to be a charity fundraiser. Mrs. Adelaide Whitmore smiled at the camera with the confidence of someone accustomed to being photographed for the society pages.

"Mrs. Whitmore?" Mrs. Duval's voice carried disbelief. "But she runs the Repository. She's dedicated to exposing corruption, not covering it up."

"Is she?" Marshal Hayes opened another file, this one considerably thicker. "We've been investigating Mrs. Adelaide Whitmore for over a year. Her 'charitable activities' have been remarkably effective at identifying people who possess inconvenient information about various criminal enterprises."

Lillian felt the pieces clicking into place with sickening clarity. "The Repository wasn't just gathering information to expose corruption. It was gathering intelligence about who knew what, so the real criminals could eliminate threats before they became dangerous."

"Precisely." Hayes spread several documents across the table. "Mrs. Whitmore has been running what we believe to be the most sophisticated criminal intelligence network in the country. She identifies potential witnesses, assesses the threats they pose, and then arranges for their… disposal… when necessary."

Penrose looked up from his notes, his face pale. "But the stories we've published, the corruption we've exposed…"

"Were carefully selected to enhance Mrs. Whitmore's reputation while eliminating her competition," Hayes explained. "She'd expose small-scale corruption to build credibility, then use that credibility to protect the larger criminal enterprises she was actually part of."

"The Hudson Valley Railway," Blackwood said grimly. "She was involved from the beginning."

Hayes nodded. "Adelaide Whitmore wasn't just an investor in the Hudson Valley expansion, she was one of the primary architects of the cover-up when the safety violations and environmental damage became too extensive to hide. Her late husband's construction company provided the substandard materials that led to the worker deaths."

The conference room fell silent as the implications sank in. Mrs. Whitmore hadn't just been protecting a conspiracy, she'd helped create it.

"Mrs. Ashworth was getting too close to the truth," Lillian said slowly. "And when Mrs. Whitmore realized that the federal investigation was inevitable, she decided to eliminate everyone who could testify."

"But there's more." Hayes pulled out a final document, a telegram dated three days earlier. "Mrs. Whitmore didn't just order these murders. She's been systematically eliminating potential witnesses for over a decade. We've identified at least eighteen suspicious deaths over the past ten years, all ruled natural causes by compliant physicians, all involving people who possessed information about various criminal enterprises connected to Mrs. Whitmore's network."

"Eighteen people," Mrs. Duval whispered. "All

those families who believed their loved ones died naturally…"

"Were actually victims of the most sophisticated murder conspiracy in American history," Hayes finished.

A knock at the door interrupted the grim revelations. A young marshal entered and whispered something to Hayes, whose expression darkened further. "Gentlemen, ladies, we have a problem. Mrs. Whitmore has disappeared."

"What do you mean, disappeared?" Blackwood demanded.

"Her mansion on Fifth Avenue is empty. According to the household staff, she received a telegram yesterday evening and left immediately afterward, taking only a single traveling case." The marshal consulted his notes. "The telegram was unsigned, but the message was simple: 'The game is exposed. Time to leave the board.' "

Lillian felt ice in her veins. "Someone warned her."

"It appears so. Which means she knew about last night's operation before it happened." Hayes stood and began pacing the length of the conference room. "She could be anywhere by now, Canada, Mexico, even Europe if she moved quickly enough."

"No," Lillian said quietly. "She's still here."

All eyes turned to her. "What makes you so certain?" Hayes asked.

"Because Mrs. Whitmore isn't just a criminal, she's an architect. She doesn't abandon her creations; she protects them." Lillian stood and moved to the window, looking out at the city where they'd played their deadly game of cat and mouse. "The Repository, her network, her reputation—those represent decades of work. She won't just walk away."

"Then where is she?" Penrose asked.

Lillian turned back to the group, her mind

working through the possibilities. "Where would someone go if they needed to destroy evidence, eliminate remaining threats, and still maintain the possibility of returning to their old life once the immediate danger passed?"

"The Repository," Mrs. Duval said suddenly. "She's gone back to destroy the records, eliminate the evidence of her network."

"And anyone who might connect her to the murders," Blackwood added grimly.

Marshal Hayes was already moving toward the door. "How many people knew the location of this Repository?"

"Everyone who was there the other night," Lillian replied. "Miss Cho, the other members we met…"

"She's going to kill them all," Mrs. Duval said, her voice hollow with realization. "Everyone who can testify about her role in the conspiracy."

Hayes turned to his subordinate. "Get every available marshal. We're going to need—"

"No." Lillian's voice cut through the marshal's orders. "Too many federal agents will spook her. She'll disappear completely, and we'll never find her."

"What are you suggesting?"

"The same thing that worked last night. A small group, moving quietly, with the advantage of knowing exactly what we're walking into." Lillian looked at her unlikely allies, the Irish detective who'd risked his career for justice, the society matron who'd discovered her own courage, and the journalist who' d chosen truth over safety.

"Mrs. Whitmore thinks she's eliminated all the threats to her operation," she continued. "She doesn't know we survived last night, doesn't know we've connected her to the murders. If we move quickly and quietly…"

"We can catch her in the act of destroying evidence," Blackwood finished.

Hayes shook his head. "I can't authorize civilians to—"

"You're not authorizing anything," Lillian interrupted. "We're simply concerned citizens checking on the welfare of friends who might be in danger."

The marshal stared at her for a long moment, then nodded slowly. "And if concerned citizens happened to discover evidence of federal crimes in progress…"

"They'd have a civic duty to report it to the proper authorities," Penrose said with a slight smile.

"Who would, naturally, respond immediately," Hayes agreed.

As they prepared to leave the courthouse, Lillian felt the familiar mixture of fear and excitement that had driven her through the past four days. Mrs. Whitmore might be the most dangerous criminal they'd yet encountered, but she was also the last piece of the puzzle.

Once they brought her to justice, the conspiracy that had begun with Mrs. Ashworth's death would finally be exposed completely. The only question was whether they would all survive long enough to see justice done.

Outside, Manhattan was waking up to what would become one of the most significant days in its criminal history. But in the hidden chambers beneath the city, a different kind of awakening was about to occur, one that would determine whether truth or corruption would ultimately prevail.

The final game was about to begin.

The hidden entrance to the Repository stood ajar when they arrived, a detail that sent ice through Lillian's veins. In their previous visits, the concealed door had been meticulously secured. Mrs. Whitmore's network had survived through careful attention to such details. An open door meant either carelessness born of desperation, or a trap.

"She knows we're coming," Detective Blackwood whispered, his hand resting on his service revolver.

"Of course she does," Lillian replied grimly. "Mrs. Whitmore has been anticipating our moves since this began. The question is whether she's prepared for what we've become."

They'd approached through the maze of alleys that Mrs. Duval now navigated with the confidence of someone who'd learned Manhattan's hidden geography through necessity. Behind them, at carefully measured distances, federal marshals moved through parallel routes. If Mrs. Whitmore tried to escape, she'd find her exits blocked.

The corridor beyond the entrance was eerily silent. The warm carpets and elegant wallpaper that had seemed welcoming before now felt oppressive, like the decorated chambers of some predatory creature's lair. Gas lamps flickered irregularly, casting dancing shadows that made every corner potentially dangerous.

"The main chamber," Mrs. Duval breathed, pointing toward the familiar circular room ahead.

As they approached, Lillian could hear voices, Mrs. Whitmore's cultured tones rising above softer responses that carried fear and confusion. The Repository's other members were still alive, but clearly in distress.

"… unfortunate necessity," Mrs. Whitmore was saying as they crept closer. "The federal investigation has forced certain… adjustments… to our operations."

Lillian peered around the doorframe into the main chamber. The scene that greeted her was both familiar and horrifying. The Repository's members sat around the mahogany table as they had during previous meetings, but now their hands were bound, and several armed men stood guard around the room's perimeter. Mrs. Whitmore paced before the wall of journals and ledgers that contained the accumulated secrets of Manhattan's elite.

"You see," Mrs. Whitmore continued, her voice carrying the reasonable tone of someone explaining a simple business decision, "the Repository has served its purpose admirably. We've identified threats, eliminated obstacles, and maintained the proper order of things for over a decade. But all good things must come to an end."

Miss Evelina Cho, the tea shop owner whose

coded messages had started their investigation, looked up with defiant eyes despite her bonds. "You're talking about murder, Adelaide. You're talking about killing innocent people to protect criminals."

"Innocent?" Mrs. Whitmore laughed, the sound carrying genuine amusement. "My dear Evelina, none of us are innocent. We've all profited from information that destroyed lives, ruined careers, and shifted the balance of power in this city. The only difference is that some of us understood the true nature of the game we were playing."

She gestured toward the bound Repository members with theatrical grandeur. "You believed you were serving justice by exposing corruption. How delightfully naive. You were actually serving me by identifying exactly which secrets were dangerous enough to require… management."

Lillian felt Blackwood tense beside her, but she placed a restraining hand on his arm. They needed to understand the full scope of Mrs. Whitmore's operation before acting.

"The Hudson Valley Railway was just the beginning," Mrs. Whitmore continued, moving toward a cabinet that Lillian recognized as containing the most sensitive documents. "Over the years, we've protected investments, eliminated whistle-blowers, and maintained the proper social order. The eighteen deaths Marshal Hayes mentioned? That's only the ones he knows about."

She pulled out a leather-bound ledger and opened it on the table. "The complete record of our activities would show forty-three successful… interventions… over the past decade. Each one carefully planned, expertly executed, and officially ruled accidental or natural."

"Forty-three people," Penrose whispered behind Lillian, his journalist's instincts horrified by the scope of the conspiracy.

Mrs. Whitmore began pulling documents from the filing cabinets, stacking them in the center of the room. "But the federal investigation threatens to expose everything. So we must… restructure… our operations. The Repository and its members must be eliminated to protect the larger network."

"What larger network?" Miss Cho demanded.

"Oh, my dear, did you think Manhattan was the extent of our activities? We have similar operations in Boston, Philadelphia, Chicago, San Francisco. The Repository was merely the New York branch of a much more extensive organization." Mrs. Whitmore's smile was coldly triumphant. "Eliminating you people will be regrettable, but it will preserve operations that generate millions of dollars annually."

She produced a can of kerosene and began splashing it over the accumulated documents. "A tragic fire, caused by faulty gas lamps. The building will be a total loss, along with everyone inside. By the time investigators sort through the wreckage, I'll be in Europe, establishing our next operational center."

This was their moment. Lillian looked at her companions and saw the same grim determination reflected in their faces. They'd come too far and lost too much to let Mrs. Whitmore escape justice.

"I'm afraid your travel plans will have to be postponed, Mrs. Whitmore," Lillian said, stepping into the chamber with her hands raised but her voice steady.

Mrs. Whitmore spun toward them, her composure cracking for the first time since Lillian had known her. "Miss Cross! How delightfully persistent of you. And Detective Blackwood, Mrs. Duval, Mr. Penrose… such a pleasure to see you all again."

Her armed guards were already moving, weapons drawn and trained on the new arrivals. But Mrs. Whitmore held up a hand, stopping them.

"Please, gentlemen, no need for violence just yet. I'm curious to hear how our amateur investigators managed to survive last night's activities." Her eyes glittered with predatory intelligence. "Though I suspect their survival was less about competence and more about the Morrison brothers' incompetence."

"The Morrison brothers told us everything," Blackwood said, his Irish accent thick with anger. "About the murders, the cover-ups, your role in orchestrating it all."

"Did they? How unfortunate for them. I do hope their stay in federal custody is… comfortable." Mrs. Whitmore's smile carried no warmth. "But their confessions hardly matter now. Within the hour, this building will be ash, and you'll all be casualties of another tragic accident."

She gestured to one of her guards, who produced a syringe that Lillian recognized with cold horror, the same medical implement that had killed Mrs. Ashworth and Mr. Pemberton.

"Strychnine is such an efficient poison," Mrs. Whitmore mused.

"Quick, relatively painless if administered properly, and virtually undetectable in fire-damaged remains. You'll simply be overcome by smoke before the flames reach you."

"Except we're not alone," Mrs. Duval said with quiet confidence.

Mrs. Whitmore's expression flickered with uncertainty. "What do you mean?"

"Federal marshals," Lillian replied. "Surrounding this building, blocking every exit. Your network might extend beyond Manhattan, Mrs. Whitmore, but your freedom ends here."

For the first time, Mrs. Whitmore looked genuinely concerned. She moved to one of the chamber's windows, peering through the narrow glass at the alleys beyond. Whatever she saw there made her face pale.

"You're bluffing," she said, but her voice lacked conviction.

"Am I?" Lillian took a step closer.

"Marshal Hayes has been building a federal case against you for over a year. The Morrison brothers' confessions simply provided the final evidence he needed. Your only choice now is how you want this to end, in custody, or in a shootout that will accomplish nothing except getting more people killed."

Mrs. Whitmore stared at her for a long moment, her mind clearly calculating possibilities and probabilities. Around the room, her guards shifted nervously, sensing their leader's uncertainty.

"You know what I find most interesting about this situation?" Mrs. Whitmore said finally, her composure returning with disturbing speed. "You actually believe you've won."

She reached into her coat and produced a small device that looked like a pocket watch. "But you've forgotten something crucial about criminal organizations, Miss Cross. We always have contingency plans."

The device in her hand began ticking audibly, and Lillian realized with horror what it was—a timer connected to incendiary charges that would turn the Repository into an inferno within minutes.

"You have exactly five minutes to escape this building before it becomes your tomb," Mrs. Whitmore announced with calm satisfaction. "Use that time wisely."

As the timer continued its relentless countdown, Lillian understood that their final confrontation with Mrs. Whitmore would be a race against time itself—with the lives of everyone in the Repository hanging in the balance.

The game had reached its ultimate move, and failure would mean death for them all

Four minutes and thirty seconds. The timer's relentless ticking filled the Repository's main chamber like a mechanical heartbeat counting down to death. Lillian's mind raced through their options, each one seeming more impossible than the last. The bound Repository members, Mrs. Whitmore's armed guards, the federal marshals outside who might not reach them in time, too many variables, too little time.

"Detective Blackwood," she said quietly, never taking her eyes off Mrs. Whitmore.

"The gas lamps."

Blackwood's eyes widened with understanding. The Repository's elegant lighting system wasn't just decorative, it was connected to a main gas line that ran throughout the building. If they could create the right kind of distraction…

"Mrs. Duval," Lillian continued, "when I give the signal, get to Miss Cho and the others. Cut their bonds."

"With what?" Mrs. Duval whispered.

Penrose discretely passed her a pen knife from his pocket. "Emergency journalism tool," he murmured.

Mrs. Whitmore watched their whispered preparations with amused detachment. "Four minutes," she announced, glancing at her timer. "I do hope you're not planning something heroic, Miss Cross. Heroes have such short life expectancies in my experience."

"I'm not a hero," Lillian replied, slowly reaching into her medical bag. "I'm a mortician's daughter who's tired of examining victims of your murders."

She pulled out a small vial of phosphorus solution, highly volatile, designed for chemical preservation but equally effective at creating sudden, brilliant flashes of light and heat.

"The interesting thing about gas lamps," Lillian said conversationally, "is how unpredictable they can be when the pressure changes suddenly."

Mrs. Whitmore's expression shifted from amusement to alarm. "Stop her!"

But Lillian was already moving. She hurled the phosphorus vial at the nearest gas fixture, and the chamber exploded into brilliant, blinding light. In the same instant, Blackwood yanked the gas control valve, sending pressure surging through the lines and causing every lamp in the room to flare dramatically.

Chaos erupted. Mrs. Whitmore's guards stumbled blindly through the phosphorus smoke while Mrs. Duval dove toward the bound Repository members, her pen knife working frantically at their ropes. Penrose knocked over furniture to create barriers and confusion.

"The timer!" Miss Cho shouted as her bonds fell away. "She's heading for the timer!"

Through the smoke and confusion, Lillian could see Mrs. Whitmore moving toward a side passage, not trying to escape, but attempting to reach something hidden in the chamber's shadows. The timer, Lillian realized. She was going to accelerate the countdown.

"Blackwood!" Lillian called, pointing toward the passage. The detective was already in motion, but one of Mrs. Whitmore's guards blocked his path. The two men grappled while precious seconds ticked away.

Three minutes.

Lillian sprinted after Mrs. Whitmore, following her into a narrow passage that led deeper into the Repository's hidden chambers. Behind her, she could hear the others freeing the remaining prisoners and fighting with the guards, but those sounds faded as she pursued the architect of so much death and suffering.

The passage opened into a smaller room lined with filing cabinets and dominated by a complex apparatus that looked like a cross between a telegraph and a clockwork mechanism. This was Mrs. Whitmore's real control center, the heart of her criminal network.

Mrs. Whitmore stood before the device, her hands moving over switches and dials with practiced efficiency.

"Two minutes and forty seconds, Miss Cross. Even if you stop me now, you'll never evacuate everyone in time."

"Maybe not," Lillian agreed, pulling out another vial from her medical bag, this one containing a strong acid used for cleaning bone samples. "But I can make sure your network dies with us."

She threw the acid across the complex apparatus, and sparks flew as the corrosive liquid ate through wires and mechanisms. The device began smoking and sparking, its carefully calibrated systems failing in a cascade of electrical fire.

"No!" Mrs. Whitmore lunged toward the dying machine. "Do you have any idea what you've just destroyed? Communications with five cities, financial records worth millions, operational plans that took decades to develop!"

"Good," Lillian said simply.

Mrs. Whitmore spun toward her, and for the first time, Lillian saw the woman's true face—not the composed society matron or the calculating criminal mastermind, but someone consumed by rage and desperation.

"You stupid girl," Mrs. Whitmore snarled, pulling a small derringer from her coat. "You've destroyed everything for what? Justice? Morality? These are luxuries that only naive children believe in."

"Maybe," Lillian agreed, backing toward the passage entrance. "But I'd rather be a naive child than a murderer."

Mrs. Whitmore raised the derringer, but before she could fire, Detective Blackwood appeared in the doorway behind Lillian, his service revolver trained on the criminal mastermind.

"Drop the weapon, Mrs. Whitmore. It's over."

For a moment, the three of them stood frozen in tableau, Mrs. Whitmore with her derringer, Blackwood with his revolver, and Lillian caught between them. The timer's ticking seemed to grow louder, marking seconds that might be their last.

Two minutes.

"You're right, Detective," Mrs. Whitmore said suddenly, her voice returning to its cultured calm. "It is over." But instead of dropping her weapon, she turned it toward the smoking remains of her control apparatus. "If I can't have my network, no one can have the evidence it contains."

She fired a single shot into the sparking

machinery, and the entire room filled with acrid smoke as electrical fires spread to the papers and files that surrounded the destroyed device.

"The building's on fire!" someone shouted from the main chamber, Penrose's voice, carrying panic and urgency.

"Everyone out!" Blackwood commanded, grabbing Lillian's arm. "Now!"

They ran back through the passage into the main chamber, where thick smoke was already beginning to pour from the Repository's various rooms. The phosphorus fire had spread beyond Lillian's initial target, and now the entire building was becoming a deathtrap.

One minute and thirty seconds.

The Repository members were streaming toward the exit, supported by Mrs. Duval and Penrose. But Mrs. Whitmore was nowhere to be seen, she'd vanished into the smoke and chaos like the criminal ghost she'd always been.

"Where is she?" Blackwood demanded.

"There!" Miss Cho pointed toward another passage, one that led toward the building's rear exit. "She knows every hidden route in this place!"

They reached the main corridor just as the sound of splintering wood echoed through the building. Federal marshals were breaking down the main entrance, but they might be too late to catch Mrs. Whitmore before she escaped through the building's hidden passages.

Fifty seconds.

"Get everyone out the front," Lillian told Blackwood. "I'm going after her."

"Lillian, no! The building's going to explode!"

But she was already running toward the rear passages, following the route Mrs. Whitmore had taken. Behind her, she could hear Blackwood cursing in both

English and Irish as he helped evacuate the others.

The rear passage was filled with smoke, but Lillian could see a figure ahead of her, Mrs. Whitmore, moving with desperate speed toward what must be a hidden exit. The woman who'd orchestrated so much death and suffering was within reach, but the timer was counting down to an explosion that would kill them both.

Thirty seconds.

Mrs. Whitmore reached a concealed door and yanked it open, revealing an alley beyond. Freedom was just steps away. She turned back toward Lillian with a smile of cold triumph.

"Too late, Miss Cross. You chose justice over survival, and now you'll—"

Her words were cut off as Marshal Hayes appeared in the alley beyond the door, his weapon drawn and federal agents flanking him on both sides.

"Adelaide Whitmore, you're under arrest for conspiracy to commit murder, racketeering, and violation of federal statutes."

Mrs. Whitmore's face went white. Trapped between Lillian and the federal agents, she had nowhere left to run.

Twenty seconds.

"The building's going to explode!" Lillian shouted to the marshals. "Everyone needs to get clear!"

Hayes grabbed Mrs. Whitmore's arm and pulled her away from the building as his agents surrounded her. Lillian ran for the exit, her lungs burning from smoke and her heart pounding as the timer reached its final countdown.

Ten seconds.

She burst from the building into the alley, where strong hands. Blackwood's hands, caught her and pulled her away from the Repository's entrance.

Five seconds.

They ran toward the street, where the other survivors were gathered at what they hoped was a safe distance.

Three.

Two.

One.

The Repository exploded in a ball of fire that lit up the Manhattan dawn like a second sunrise. The building collapsed in on itself, taking with it the accumulated secrets of a decade and the physical evidence of Mrs. Whitmore's criminal network.

But the woman herself stood in federal custody, surrounded by marshals and facing a list of charges that would ensure she never again threatened innocent lives.

As the smoke cleared and the fire department arrived to contain the blaze, Lillian found herself standing next to Detective Blackwood, both of them alive and whole despite everything they'd endured.

"So," Blackwood said, his Irish accent soft with exhaustion and relief. "What does the undertaker's daughter do for an encore?"

Lillian looked around at the scene, federal agents arresting criminals, Repository members giving statements about the conspiracy they'd unknowingly served, journalists documenting the exposure of Manhattan's most sophisticated criminal network.

"I think," she said slowly, "the undertaker's daughter might consider a career change. Maybe something in criminal investigation."

Blackwood's smile was warm despite the soot covering his face. "I might know someone who could help with that."

As the sun rose fully over Manhattan, casting long shadows through the smoke that marked the end of Mrs. Whitmore's criminal empire, Lillian Cross realized that her story was just beginning. She'd started this adventure as someone who examined the dead to understand how they'd died.

Now she was someone who fought for the living, to ensure they had the chance to keep living.

It was, she thought, a much better way to spend one's time.

*Three months later*

The brass nameplate on the door read "Cross & Associates - Private Investigators," and Lillian couldn't help but smile every time she saw it. The office was modest, two rooms above a baker's shop in a respectable part of Manhattan, but it was theirs.

Detective Blackwood, Nathaniel, she'd finally begun calling him, looked up from the case files spread across his desk as she entered with their afternoon tea.

"Any word from the federal prosecutors?" she asked.

"Mrs. Whitmore was sentenced this morning. Life imprisonment without possibility of parole." His satisfaction was evident. "The Morrison brothers received twenty-five years each, and the federal investigation has identified criminal networks in four other cities based on the evidence we recovered."

Through their window, Lillian could see the construction crews working to rebuild the Repository's former location. It would become a federal office building, Marshal Hayes had told them, a fitting transformation from a center of criminal intelligence to a symbol of justice.

"What about our other cases?" Nathaniel asked.

Lillian consulted her appointment book, a skill she'd learned from Miss Cho, who now ran a legitimate tea shop without any coded messaging systems. "Two insurance fraud investigations, a missing person case, and something involving suspicious circumstances at a textile factory."

"Suspicious circumstances," Nathaniel repeated with amusement. "In other words, the sort of case that attracts undertakers' daughters who can't resist investigating mysterious deaths."

"Former undertakers' daughters," Lillian corrected. "I'm a private investigator now."

"With an unusual specialty in forensic analysis."

"Someone has to speak for the dead, Nathaniel. We just make sure they're heard by the living."

A knock at their door interrupted the conversation. Mrs. Duval entered, elegant as always but now with the practical air of someone who'd discovered useful work to do.

"I have another case for you," she announced, settling into the chair they'd designated as hers. Her new role as liaison between their detective agency and Manhattan's reform movements had proved invaluable, she knew which mysteries needed solving and which powerful people needed investigating.

"What sort of case?" Lillian asked.

"Missing funds from a charity organization. The sort of charity that provides aid to immigrant families." Mrs. Duval's expression was grim. "Someone's been stealing money meant to help the people who need it most."

Lillian and Nathaniel exchanged glances. It was exactly the sort of case they'd founded their agency to handle, crimes that affected ordinary people, investigations that the official authorities might not prioritize.

"We'll take it," Lillian said without hesitation.

As Mrs. Duval provided the details of their new case, Lillian reflected on how much had changed since that October night when Mrs. Ashworth had died in Miss Cho's tea shop. She'd gained partners, skills, and a purpose that went far beyond preparing the dead for burial.

But some things hadn't changed. She still believed that the dead deserved justice, that secrets had a way of festering until exposed to light, and that the truth. No matter how dangerous or inconvenient, was always worth pursuing.

Outside their window, Manhattan continued its relentless pace of growth and change. But in the office of Cross & Associates, three unlikely partners prepared to tackle their next case, confident that whatever mysteries awaited them, they would face them together.

After all, some partnerships were forged not just in shared danger, but in shared commitment to justice.

And those partnerships, Lillian had learned, were the strongest foundation of all.

THE
GILDED CORPSE

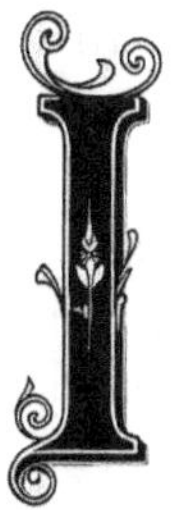

The Vandermeer mansion stood like a marble monument to American excess, its towering columns and manicured gardens declaring to all of Fifth Avenue that money could indeed buy everything, including, apparently, the silence of the Metropolitan Police.

Lillian Cross adjusted her borrowed evening gloves and tried not to feel like an impostor among Manhattan's glittering elite. The autumn charity gala swirled around her in a sea of silk, diamonds, and barely concealed gossip, but her attention remained fixed on the fountain in the mansion's rear courtyard, the same fountain where Miss Charlotte Vandermeer had been found dead three days earlier.

"Suicide, they're calling it," Detective Nathaniel Blackwood murmured beside her, his Irish accent carefully modulated for their current company.

"Distraught over a broken engagement, according to the family."

"And you believe that?" Lillian asked, watching as guests pointedly avoided the fountain area despite the warm October evening.

"I believe what the evidence tells me. And the evidence says Miss Vandermeer was murdered."

Mrs. Margaret Duval appeared at Lillian's elbow with the fluid grace of someone born to navigate society gatherings. "The family's story is that Charlotte discovered her fiancé's... indiscretions... with another woman. Threw herself into the fountain in a fit of despair."

"Wearing full mourning dress?" Lillian observed. "Rather dramatic for someone planning a wedding next month."

"Indeed. And have you noticed who's conspicuously absent from tonight's gathering?" Mrs. Duval's eyes swept the crowd with practiced assessment. "Mr. Harrison Ashford, the grieving fiancé himself."

Lillian studied the faces around them, noting the carefully neutral expressions that spoke of secrets shared and dangers avoided. These people knew something about Charlotte Vandermeer's death, but Fifth Avenue society had its own code of silence, one that made the criminal underworld look chatty by comparison.

"Miss Cross?" A young woman approached them, her face pale despite carefully applied cosmetics. "I'm Katherine Vandermeer, Charlotte's younger sister. I wondered if I might speak with you privately?"

Lillian recognized the desperate look in the girl's eyes, the same expression she'd seen on Mrs. Duval's face weeks earlier, when a society matron realized that respectability was no protection against murder.

"Of course, Miss Vandermeer."

They moved to a quieter corner of the

ballroom, away from the orchestra and the forced merriment of guests who were trying very hard not to discuss recent tragedy.

"You investigated that terrible business with Mrs. Whitmore," Katherine said without preamble. "Everyone's talking about how you exposed her criminal network."

"We had help from many people," Lillian replied carefully.

"My sister didn't kill herself." Katherine's voice was barely above a whisper, but her conviction was absolute. "Charlotte was many things, headstrong, impulsive, sometimes reckless, but she wasn't despairing. She was angry."

"Angry about what?"

"About what she'd discovered about Harrison. About what he'd gotten involved in." Katherine glanced around nervously before continuing. "The night before she died, Charlotte told me she'd found something that would 'destroy Harrison and everyone connected to him.' Those were her exact words."

Lillian felt the familiar stirring of curiosity that had led her into the Repository investigation. "What had she found?"

"I don't know. But she'd been asking questions about Harrison's business associates, his investments, his... social activities. Charlotte wasn't content to be a decorative society wife, she wanted to understand exactly what kind of man she was marrying."

"And what did she discover?"

Katherine's laugh held no humor. "That Harrison Ashford moves in circles where young women who ask too many questions have a tendency to meet with accidents."

A chill ran down Lillian's spine. "Miss Vandermeer, are you suggesting that your sister was killed because of information she'd uncovered?"

"I'm saying my sister was found drowned in our fountain wearing a mourning dress she'd never owned, with rope burns on her wrists that the police insist came from 'thrashing about in despair.'" Katherine's eyes blazed with barely controlled fury. "Charlotte was an excellent swimmer, Miss Cross. She could have gotten out of that fountain even in evening dress, even if she'd wanted to die, which she didn't."

Before Lillian could respond, a commotion near the ballroom's main entrance drew their attention. Harrison Ashford had arrived, late and clearly the worse for alcohol, his usually immaculate appearance disheveled and his eyes holding the haunted look of a man living with terrible knowledge.

"Ah," Katherine said with bitter satisfaction. "The grieving fiancé makes his entrance."

Lillian watched as Ashford moved through the crowd, noting how conversations died and resumed around him like ripples in a disturbed pond. This was a man carrying dangerous secrets, and everyone in the room seemed to know it.

"Miss Vandermeer," Lillian said quietly, "if we were to investigate your sister's death, we would need complete honesty from you. About Charlotte, about Mr. Ashford, about whatever your sister discovered that got her killed."

"You'll help us?" Hope and desperation warred in Katherine's voice.

"If there's justice to be found, we'll find it." Lillian's promise carried the weight of experience earned through recent trials. "But be warned, the truth about your sister's death may destroy more than just Mr. Ashford's reputation."

Katherine Vandermeer's smile was sharp as winter steel. "Miss Cross, my sister is dead because someone thought her life was worth less than their secrets. I want those secrets exposed, regardless of who gets destroyed in the process."

As Lillian watched Harrison Ashford stumble toward the fountain courtyard, drawn, perhaps, to the scene of his crime—she realized that the investigation into Charlotte Vandermeer's death would take her into even more dangerous territory than Mrs. Whitmore's criminal network.

The corruption of the poor was one thing. But the corruption of the powerful, protected by wealth and social position, would prove far more deadly to expose.

Still, as she'd told Mrs. Duval weeks earlier, some truths were worth any risk to uncover.

And Charlotte Vandermeer's truth was calling to her from the bottom of a Fifth Avenue fountain, demanding justice from the only people brave enough, or foolish enough, to listen.

The morning after the charity gala, Lillian stood in the Vandermeer's rear courtyard, studying the fountain where Charlotte had died with the same methodical attention she'd once reserved for examination tables in her father's preparation room. The fountain was an ostentatious affair, Italian marble carved with cherubs and sea creatures, water cascading from multiple tiers into a basin that couldn't have been more than three feet deep at its center.

"An excellent swimmer," she murmured, echoing Katherine's words from the previous night. "She could have stood up at any point."

Detective Blackwood crouched near the fountain's edge, examining the marble with practiced attention. "No blood, no signs of a struggle. If she was held under, whoever did it was strong enough to control her without leaving obvious marks."

"Or she was already unconscious when she

entered the water." Lillian pulled out her notebook, sketching the scene with quick, precise strokes. The courtyard was surrounded by tall windows from the mansion's first and second floors, dozens of potential witnesses, yet no one had reported seeing or hearing anything unusual.

"Miss Cross, Mr. Blackwood." Mrs. Cornelia Vandermeer's voice cut through the morning air like a knife through silk. "I wasn't aware you'd been given permission to examine my daughter's... the fountain."

The Vandermeer matriarch stood on the terrace steps, resplendent in black mourning dress that probably cost more than most families earned in a year. Her face bore the careful neutrality of someone who'd learned to hide emotions behind layers of social propriety.

"Mrs. Vandermeer." Lillian straightened, tucking her notebook away. "Katherine asked us to—"

"My youngest daughter is distraught and not thinking clearly," Mrs. Vandermeer interrupted smoothly. "The police have already ruled Charlotte's death a suicide. There's nothing more to investigate."

"With respect, ma'am, your daughter drowned in three feet of water," Blackwood said, his Irish accent thickening slightly with frustration. "That's difficult to accomplish accidentally, and even more difficult if the person was a strong swimmer."

"Are you suggesting my daughter was murdered, Detective?" Mrs. Vandermeer's tone could have frozen the fountain's water. "How... sensational. I suppose next you'll be telling me Charlotte was involved in some sordid scandal that led to her demise?"

Lillian caught the deliberate manipulation in the woman's words—framing any investigation as scandalous gossip rather than pursuit of justice. "We're suggesting that there are inconsistencies in the official verdict that warrant further examination."

"The only inconsistency I see is my younger daughter's refusal to accept reality." Mrs. Vandermeer descended the terrace steps with the bearing of a queen granting audience to peasants. "Charlotte was heartbroken over Harrison's betrayal. She took her own life in a moment of emotional distress. It's tragic, but not mysterious."

"Then you won't mind if we examine the mourning dress she was wearing when she died," Lillian said calmly. "Katherine mentioned it wasn't one Charlotte owned."

Mrs. Vandermeer's composure flickered for just an instant, a subtle tightening around her eyes that suggested the question had struck a nerve. "The dress was borrowed from a friend. Charlotte was preparing for contingencies. She knew her engagement was ending."

"Which friend?"

"I don't recall. Charlotte had many acquaintances." The dismissal was absolute. "Now, if you'll excuse me, I have arrangements to finalize. My husband and I would appreciate it if you would respect our family's privacy during this difficult time."

She swept back into the mansion, leaving Lillian and Blackwood standing in the courtyard like dismissed servants.

"She's lying," Blackwood said flatly once Mrs. Vandermeer was out of earshot.

"About the dress, certainly. Possibly about everything else." Lillian returned her attention to the fountain, studying the angles and sight lines. "But why? If Charlotte truly committed suicide, what does the family gain by obstructing an investigation?"

"Protection from scandal. You heard Mrs. Vandermeer, any investigation is 'sensational gossip' that reflects poorly on the family." Blackwood stood and moved to examine the windows overlooking the courtyard. "Though I'll admit, there's protecting the family reputation and then there's actively covering up a murder."

A soft footfall on the terrace made them both turn. Katherine Vandermeer appeared, dressed in simple black with none of her mother's elaborate mourning attire. In the morning light, she looked younger than her nineteen years, dark circles under her eyes suggesting sleepless nights.

"Mother sent you away, didn't she?" Katherine's voice was resigned rather than surprised. "She's been doing that to everyone who asks uncomfortable questions. The servants, Charlotte's friends, even the police detective who initially responded to the… discovery."

"Miss Vandermeer," Lillian said gently, "we need to know everything about the morning your sister was found. Even details that seem insignificant."

Katherine moved to one of the wrought-iron benches that dotted the courtyard and sat heavily, as if the weight of memory was too much to bear standing. "I found her. At dawn. I couldn't sleep, so I came down for air, and…" Her voice trailed off, and she stared at the fountain as if seeing something invisible to others.

Lillian sat beside her, while Blackwood maintained a respectful distance. "Take your time."

"She was floating face-down in the water, wearing that black dress. At first, I thought it was a trick of the light, that it couldn't be Charlotte because she would never wear something so... severe." Katherine's hands twisted in her lap. "I screamed, and the servants came running. Father pulled her from the water, and someone sent for Dr. Morrison."

"How long between when you found her and when the doctor arrived?"

"Perhaps thirty minutes? Father tried to revive her, but…" Katherine's voice broke. "Dr. Morrison examined her for maybe five minutes before pronouncing her dead. Suicide, he said. Tragic but clear."

"Did you see the rope burns on her wrists then?" Blackwood asked.

Katherine nodded. "I asked about them. Dr. Morrison said they were from Charlotte thrashing in the water, desperate movements before drowning. But I've seen Charlotte swim in rough ocean surf at Newport, she was graceful even in crisis. Those marks looked like…" She paused, seeming to search for words. "Like someone had bound her."

Lillian felt the familiar tightening in her chest that came with recognizing a truth others preferred to ignore. "Did anyone touch the body besides your father and Dr. Morrison?"

"Mother insisted on… arranging her. Charlotte's hair, her dress. She said our daughter shouldn't be seen in disarray." Katherine's laugh was bitter. "Always concerned with appearances, even in death."

"And the dress? Did your mother say anything about where it came from?"

"Only that Charlotte must have borrowed it. But I searched Charlotte's room afterward, every closet, every trunk. There's no record of her borrowing mourning clothes from anyone." Katherine met Lillian's eyes with desperate intensity. "Charlotte was planning a wedding, Miss Cross. Why would she borrow a mourning dress?"

Before Lillian could respond, Theodore Vandermeer appeared on the terrace, his imposing figure backlit by the mansion's interior lights. The railroad baron carried himself with the confident authority of someone accustomed to commanding both boardrooms and households.

"Katherine, I believe your mother asked you to rest." His voice was firm but not unkind. "And Miss

Cross, Detective Blackwood, I'm afraid I must ask you to leave. My wife is quite distressed by your continued presence."

"Mr. Vandermeer," Blackwood began, "we're simply trying to—"

"I know what you're trying to do, Detective. And while I appreciate your… diligence… the matter is closed." Vandermeer descended the steps with measured deliberation. "Charlotte's death was a tragedy, but it was not a crime. The police have made their determination, and we must respect that verdict."

"Even if it's wrong?" Lillian stood, facing the older man with more boldness than she felt. "Even if your daughter was murdered?"

Something flickered in Vandermeer's eyes, fear, perhaps, or recognition. But it vanished so quickly that Lillian couldn't be certain she'd seen anything at all.

"Young woman, I understand you've built a certain reputation for… unconventional investigations. But this is not some tenement murder or criminal conspiracy." His tone was condescending, dismissive. "This is a family matter, and we will handle it within our family."

"Charlotte deserves justice," Katherine said quietly, standing beside Lillian in a show of solidarity.

"Charlotte deserves peace," her father countered. "And she won't find it if her name is dragged through scandal and speculation." He turned his attention back to Lillian and Blackwood. "I'm asking you politely to respect our wishes. But if necessary, I can make your continued investigation… difficult. I have friends in the police department, the district attorney's office, and the mayor's inner circle. I'd prefer not to use those connections against a well-meaning detective and a mortician's daughter, but I will if you force my hand."

The threat was delivered with the casual

certainty of a man who'd never doubted his power to shape circumstances to his preference. Lillian felt the familiar sting of being reminded of her place, not through violence or crude intimidation, but through the simple reality of social hierarchy.

"We understand, Mr. Vandermeer," she said, though every instinct screamed to argue. "We'll leave."

As they collected their things and made their way toward the courtyard's side exit, Katherine caught Lillian's arm. "Don't give up," she whispered urgently. "Charlotte's journal—I'll get it to you. Tonight. The servants' entrance, after midnight."

Lillian nodded slightly, not daring to speak where Theodore Vandermeer might overhear. They left through the side gate, emerging onto Fifth Avenue where their modest carriage waited, a stark contrast to the gleaming coaches that served the mansion's family and guests.

"Well," Blackwood said once they were safely away from the Vandermeer estate, "that was a thorough dismissal."

"They're hiding something," Lillian replied, already turning the pieces over in her mind. "Both parents were too quick to shut down questions, too eager to accept the suicide verdict."

"Question is whether they're hiding a murder or just protecting the family from scandal." Blackwood loosened his collar, clearly relieved to be away from Fifth Avenue's suffocating propriety. "Could be they genuinely believe Charlotte killed herself but don't want the details examined too closely."

"Or they know exactly what happened and are terrified of the truth coming out." Lillian pulled out her notebook, reviewing the sketches she'd made of the fountain and courtyard. "Katherine said she'd bring us Charlotte's journal tonight. Whatever Charlotte discovered about Harrison must be documented there."

"Assuming the family hasn't already destroyed it."

"Katherine would have mentioned if it were gone. She's keeping it hidden somewhere her parents can't find it." Lillian looked up from her notes, meeting Blackwood's eyes. "We need to find out more about Harrison Ashford's business dealings. Whatever Charlotte discovered, it was dangerous enough to kill for."

Blackwood nodded slowly. "I'll check with my contacts in the financial district. See what rumors are circulating about Ashford and his associates."

"And I'll consult with Mrs. Duval. She moves in circles where this sort of information flows beneath the surface of polite conversation." Lillian felt the familiar mix of excitement and trepidation that came with pursuing a case against powerful opposition. "The Vandermeers may have friends in high places, but so do we."

As their carriage rattled through the morning streets toward their office, Lillian couldn't shake the image of Charlotte Vandermeer floating in three feet of water, wearing a mourning dress that didn't belong to her. A woman who'd asked too many questions and paid for her curiosity with her life.

Whatever secrets Harrison Ashford was hiding, they would find them. And whatever forces had conspired to silence Charlotte Vandermeer, they would face them.

Justice, Lillian had learned, wasn't something granted by the powerful to the powerless. It was something that had to be taken, fought for, and earned through persistence and courage.

Charlotte Vandermeer would have her justice, even if Fifth Avenue society preferred she stay silently buried.

Mrs. Margaret Duval's townhouse occupied a respectable address between the ostentatious wealth of Fifth Avenue and the more modest neighborhoods where people like Lillian lived. It was the perfect location for a woman who straddled social worlds—wealthy enough to be taken seriously by the elite, but pragmatic enough to understand that respectability didn't equal morality.

The butler who answered Lillian's knock recognized her immediately and showed her to Mrs. Duval's private study without the usual formalities. Since their partnership had begun after the Whitmore affair, Lillian had become something of a regular visitor, though she suspected the servants still whispered about the mortician's daughter who called on their mistress for business rather than social purposes.

Mrs. Duval looked up from a stack of

correspondence, her silver hair perfectly arranged despite the early afternoon hour. "Lillian! I wasn't expecting you until this evening. Has something happened with the Vandermeer investigation?"

"The family has made it abundantly clear that we're not welcome." Lillian settled into the chair across from Mrs. Duval's desk, grateful to be in a space where she didn't have to constantly prove her right to exist. "Theodore Vandermeer threatened to use his political connections to obstruct us if we continue asking questions."

"How predictable." Mrs. Duval set aside her letters with a sigh. "The wealthy always assume their money makes them untouchable. What can I do to help?"

"Tell me about Harrison Ashford. Everything Fifth Avenue knows but won't say openly."

Mrs. Duval's expression grew thoughtful as she moved to a cabinet and retrieved a leather-bound journal, not unlike the one Lillian kept for case notes, but filled instead with social observations and carefully documented gossip.

"Harrison Ashford," she began, flipping through pages covered in her neat handwriting. "Twenty-eight years old, only son of the late James Ashford, who made his fortune in shipping and imports. The family wealth is substantial but not quite as secure as they'd like people to believe."

"Meaning?"

"Meaning Harrison's father was better at spending money than making it. When he died five years ago, he left his son with impressive social standing but a somewhat diminished financial portfolio." Mrs. Duval consulted her notes. "Harrison has been attempting to rebuild the family fortune through various investments, some more successful than others."

Lillian pulled out her own notebook. "What sort

of investments?"

"That's where things become interesting. Publicly, Harrison is involved in respectable ventures, municipal bonds, established businesses, real estate. But there have been rumors about his more… creative… endeavors."

"What kind of rumors?"

Mrs. Duval hesitated, choosing her words carefully. "Stock manipulation schemes targeting immigrant investors who don't understand American financial systems. Insurance arrangements that seem to benefit from unfortunate accidents. Business partnerships with men whose fortunes came from decidedly questionable sources."

"You're describing criminal activity," Lillian said flatly.

"I'm describing what's whispered at charity galas when the champagne flows freely." Mrs. Duval's tone was precise. "Nothing provable, nothing documented, but enough smoke to suggest fire. Harrison moves in circles of wealthy young men who believe that rules are for people without connections."

"Who else is in these circles?"

Mrs. Duval consulted her journal again. "Robert Thornton, son of a banking family, known for aggressive business practices that skirt legality. William Hartley, real estate developer who's made enemies among tenement residents. Charles Pemberton, whose family shipping business has been investigated multiple times for customs violations." She paused. "And that's just the names I know. There are likely others who are more discrete about their associations."

Lillian wrote quickly, connecting pieces in her mind. "Charlotte Vandermeer was investigating Harrison's business dealings. If she discovered evidence of actual crimes rather than just rumors…"

"She became a liability that needed to be

eliminated." Mrs. Duval closed her journal with a decisive snap. "Which raises a troubling question, did Harrison kill her himself, or did he have help?"

"Katherine mentioned that Charlotte said whatever she'd discovered would 'destroy Harrison and everyone connected to him.' That suggests a conspiracy rather than one man acting alone."

"Then we're not just investigating a murder. We're potentially exposing a criminal network operating within Manhattan's elite society." Mrs. Duval's expression was grim. "Lillian, you understand what that means? These aren't desperate criminals from the tenements. These are men with resources, connections, and the protection that comes from social position."

"The same protections that Mrs. Whitmore enjoyed before we exposed her."

"And look how many people died before we succeeded in bringing her to justice." Mrs. Duval moved to her window, gazing out at the street below. "I want to help you, my dear. But I need you to acknowledge the danger we're walking into."

Lillian joined her at the window, watching carriages pass on the street below, each one carrying people whose lives were shaped by the invisible networks of power and privilege that governed Manhattan society.

"Charlotte Vandermeer is dead because she asked uncomfortable questions," Lillian said quietly. "If we don't pursue this investigation, we're telling every woman in this city that curiosity is dangerous, that truth matters less than social stability, that powerful men can murder with impunity as long as they maintain the proper façade."

"When you put it that way, I suppose we have no choice." Mrs. Duval turned back to face her with a slight smile. "What do you need from me?"

"Information about Harrison's associates. Who

they are, where they meet, what businesses they're involved in." Lillian consulted her notes. "And anything you can discover about the mourning dress Charlotte was wearing when she died. Someone provided that dress, and I'd like to know who."

"The dress is an interesting detail." Mrs. Duval returned to her desk and pulled out a fresh sheet of paper. "Mourning attire is quite specific, proper society women have strict rules about fabric, cut, and ornamentation. If I can determine the style and quality of the dress, I might be able to identify which dressmaker created it."

"And from there, trace who purchased it?"

"Or at least narrow down the possibilities. Elite dressmakers keep detailed records of their clients." Mrs. Duval began writing names. "Leave that aspect to me. I can make inquiries that won't raise suspicions, just a society matron updating her wardrobe."

A knock at the study door interrupted them. The butler entered with an apologetic expression. "Pardon the interruption, madam, but there's a gentleman here to see Miss Cross. A Detective Blackwood? He says it's urgent."

Lillian and Mrs. Duval exchanged glances. "Show him in," Mrs. Duval instructed.

Nathaniel Blackwood entered moments later, his expression carrying the particular intensity that meant he'd discovered something significant. He nodded respectfully to Mrs. Duval before turning his attention to Lillian.

"I've just come from the financial district," he said without preamble. "The rumors about Harrison Ashford are worse than we suspected."

"How much worse?" Lillian asked.

"There's a federal investigation building. Quietly, not officially announced yet, but several of my contacts mentioned that Treasury agents have been asking questions about stock manipulation schemes targeting immigrant communities." Blackwood pulled out his own notebook. "Harrison Ashford's name keeps appearing in connection with these investigations, along with those associates Mrs. Duval likely already mentioned."

"Treasury agents?" Mrs. Duval's eyebrows rose. "That's considerably more serious than simple fraud."

"It suggests organized criminal activity on a significant scale." Blackwood flipped through his notes. "From what I've gathered, the scheme works like this: wealthy investors identify recent immigrants who've managed to save money, then offer them 'guaranteed' investment opportunities. The money goes into legitimate-looking ventures that are actually fronts. By the time the immigrants realize they've been swindled, the money has been moved through so many channels that it's nearly impossible to trace."

"And when the victims complain?" Lillian asked, though she suspected she already knew the answer.

"They're told their investments simply failed, bad luck, not fraud. Most don't speak English well enough to navigate the legal system, and they're afraid that making accusations against wealthy Americans will result in deportation." Blackwood's frustration was evident in his voice. "It's a nearly perfect crime because the victims are too vulnerable to fight back."

Mrs. Duval had gone pale. "How much money are we talking about?"

"Conservative estimates suggest hundreds of thousands of dollars over the past three years. Possibly more."

The room fell silent as they all processed the implications. This wasn't just a murder investigation, it was potentially the exposure of a massive criminal conspiracy that victimized the city's most vulnerable residents.

"Charlotte discovered this," Lillian said finally.

"She was investigating Harrison's business dealings and found evidence of the fraud."

"Which means her death wasn't just about protecting Harrison's reputation." Blackwood's expression was grim. "It was about protecting a criminal enterprise worth hundreds of thousands of dollars and involving multiple wealthy families."

"Families who would have considerable motivation to ensure Charlotte's silence," Mrs. Duval added.

Lillian's mind raced through possibilities. "Katherine is bringing us Charlotte's journal tonight. If Charlotte documented what she discovered, we'll have evidence that connects Harrison and his associates to the fraud."

"Evidence that would destroy them," Blackwood said. "And evidence worth killing to suppress."

"Then we need to be extremely careful about tonight's meeting." Mrs. Duval stood and moved to her desk, writing rapidly. "Katherine is in danger simply by possessing that journal. Once we have it, she'll be in even greater danger because the conspirators will know she's actively working against them."

"Can we offer her protection?" Lillian asked.

"Not officially," Blackwood replied. "I'm just a detective investigating what's officially been ruled a suicide. I have no authority to assign protection to a wealthy young woman against her family's wishes."

"Then we'll have to improvise." Mrs. Duval finished writing and handed Lillian a note. "This is the address of a boarding house I own in a respectable neighborhood. If Katherine needs to leave her family home quickly, she can go there. The landlady is trustworthy and won't ask uncomfortable questions."

Lillian took the note gratefully. "Thank you."

"One more thing," Blackwood said, his tone

suggesting he'd saved the most troubling information for last. "I asked some questions about Dr. Morrison, the physician who examined Charlotte's body."

"And?"

"He's on retainer for several wealthy families, including the Vandermeers. He's known for providing… convenient… medical opinions when families prefer to avoid scandal."

The implications hit Lillian like a physical blow. "You're saying he deliberately misdiagnosed Charlotte's death as suicide?"

"I'm saying he had considerable financial incentive to reach whatever conclusion the family preferred." Blackwood's jaw tightened. "It's not proof of conspiracy, but it's another piece that doesn't fit the official narrative."

Mrs. Duval sank back into her chair. "This is bigger than we initially suspected. We're not just investigating a murder, we're potentially exposing corruption that reaches from immigrant tenements to Fifth Avenue mansions, from street-level fraud to compromised physicians."

"Which is exactly why we need to be careful," Lillian said, forcing herself to think strategically rather than emotionally. "We meet Katherine at midnight, retrieve the journal, and then we need somewhere safe to examine it. Somewhere the conspirators won't think to look."

"Not your office," Blackwood said immediately. "Too obvious."

"Not here either," Mrs. Duval agreed. "I'm known to be your associate, they'll watch this house if they're suspicious."

"My father's funeral parlor," Lillian suggested. "No one would think to look there, and we'd have privacy to work through the night if necessary."

Blackwood nodded slowly. "It's morbid, but

practical. And your father?"

"Sleeps on the upper floor. As long as we're quiet in the preparation rooms, he won't be disturbed." Lillian checked her pocket watch—six hours until midnight. "We should all rest before tonight. If Charlotte's journal contains what we think it does, we'll be working through the morning to build a case."

As they finalized their plans and prepared to separate until the midnight meeting, Lillian felt the familiar weight of an investigation reaching its critical phase. They were committed now, moving forward into territory where powerful people would fight desperately to protect their secrets.

Charlotte Vandermeer had died pursuing the truth. Lillian was determined to ensure that her death would mean something, that the conspiracy she'd uncovered would be exposed, and that the powerful men who'd silenced her would finally face consequences.

Justice for Charlotte, and justice for every immigrant family they'd victimized.

The real investigation was about to begin.

Midnight on Fifth Avenue was a different world than the bustling daylight hours. The grand mansions stood dark and silent, their inhabitants asleep behind curtained windows, while the street lamps cast pools of yellow light that seemed to emphasize the shadows between them. Lillian pressed herself against the wall near the Vandermeer mansion's servants' entrance, acutely aware of how exposed they were despite the late hour.

"She's late," Detective Blackwood murmured beside her, his breath visible in the cold October air.

Lillian checked her pocket watch for the third time in as many minutes. "Only by five minutes. Perhaps she had difficulty leaving the house unnoticed."

"Or perhaps she's been discovered." Blackwood's hand rested near his coat pocket where Lillian knew he kept his service revolver. "We should have a contingency plan."

Before Lillian could respond, the servants' door opened a crack, and Katherine Vandermeer's pale face appeared in the gap. Even in the dim light, Lillian could see that the young woman had been crying.

"Miss Cross? Thank God." Katherine slipped through the door, clutching a leather-bound journal to her chest like a shield. "I was afraid you wouldn't come."

"What's wrong?" Lillian asked, noting how Katherine's hands trembled.

"My parents know I've been asking questions. Father confronted me after dinner, demanded to know why I was spreading rumors about Charlotte's death." Katherine's voice shook. "He said if I continued to make trouble, he'd send me to our Newport estate until I 'recovered from my grief and came to my senses.'"

"That's essentially imprisonment," Blackwood said grimly.

"I know." Katherine thrust the journal toward Lillian. "Take this. Charlotte documented everything—Harrison's business associates, the fraud schemes, even names of specific immigrant families they'd swindled. If anything happens to me, at least the evidence will be safe."

Lillian took the journal, feeling the weight of it, not just physical weight, but the burden of truth that had cost Charlotte her life. "Katherine, we have a safe place for you if you need to leave your family home. Mrs. Duval—"

"I can't." Katherine cut her off. "If I disappear, Father will use every resource he has to find me, and that would draw attention to your investigation. I have to stay and pretend to be the obedient daughter." Her smile was bitter. "At least until you have enough evidence to expose them all."

A sound from inside the house made them all freeze, footsteps, distant but approaching. Katherine's face went white.

"The night watchman. He makes rounds every hour." She backed toward the door. "You have to go. If he finds you here—"

"Wait," Lillian said urgently. "The mourning dress Charlotte was wearing. Do you know where it came from?"

"I don't know, but…" Katherine paused, thinking rapidly. "Charlotte mentioned something a few days before she died. She'd found a receipt in Harrison's study for a dress shop on Madison Avenue. She thought it was strange because Harrison had no sisters, no female relatives who would need mourning clothes."

"Do you remember the shop's name?"

"Madame Celeste's, I think. Or maybe Madame Colette's?" Katherine glanced nervously over her shoulder. "Charlotte thought he'd bought the dress for another woman, that it proved he was being unfaithful. But now…"

"Now it suggests premeditation," Blackwood finished. "He bought the dress before Charlotte died, planning to stage her suicide in mourning attire."

The footsteps inside grew louder, accompanied by the jingle of keys. Katherine's panic was evident.

"Go! Please!" She slipped back through the door and closed it softly, leaving Lillian and Blackwood alone in the shadows.

They moved quickly away from the mansion, sticking to the darker portions of the street until they'd put several blocks between themselves and the Vandermeer estate. Only when they reached a better-lit avenue with late-night traffic did they slow their pace.

"That was too close," Blackwood said, his relief evident.

"Katherine's in danger." Lillian clutched the journal tightly. "Her father suspects she's working against him, and if Harrison and his associates discover she gave us this evidence…"

"We need to move quickly. Build a case before they have time to eliminate witnesses or destroy evidence." Blackwood checked the street around them. "Your father's funeral parlor?"

Lillian nodded. "It's the safest place to examine this without being observed."

They made their way through Manhattan's late-night streets, passing the occasional hansom cab and groups of workers ending night shifts. The city never truly slept, but it grew quieter in these hours, as if catching its breath before the chaos of morning.

Cross & Sons Funeral Parlor stood dark and silent when they arrived. Lillian used her key to let them in through the rear entrance, moving with the practiced quiet of someone who'd grown up in these rooms and knew which floorboards creaked.

The preparation room in the basement was exactly as she'd left it earlier, marble tables gleaming in the gaslight, her father's tools arranged with meticulous precision, the faint smell of carbolic acid and preservatives that had become as familiar as perfume. She lit several lamps while Blackwood secured the door behind them.

"It's strange being here in the middle of the night," he commented, looking around the basement with obvious discomfort. "Feels like we're disturbing something that should remain undisturbed."

"The dead don't mind company." Lillian cleared one of the worktables and carefully opened Charlotte's journal. "They're remarkably tolerant of investigation."

The journal was clearly Charlotte Vandermeer's, the handwriting was elegant but energetic, with occasional underlines and exclamation marks that suggested passion behind the careful documentation. The early entries were mundane observations about Harrison's business meetings and social engagements, but as Lillian flipped through the pages, the tone shifted dramatically.

"Harrison met again with Robert Thornton and William Hartley at the Union Club," one entry read. "They spoke of 'opportunities in the immigrant communities'—I thought they meant charitable work until I heard them laughing about how 'the Irish don't understand American business practices.'"

"She was suspicious from the beginning," Lillian observed, reading aloud for Blackwood's benefit.

Later entries detailed Charlotte's growing investigation. She'd followed Harrison to meetings, eavesdropped on conversations, even bribed a clerk to show her business documents.

"The fraud is systematic," Charlotte had written in increasingly urgent prose.

"They target families who've just received insurance payments or settlements from workplace accidents. Promise guaranteed returns of 20%, take the money, and then claim the investments failed. The victims are too frightened to pursue legal action, too unfamiliar with American law to know they've been swindled."

"She was thorough," Blackwood said admiringly, reading over Lillian's shoulder. "Names, dates, amounts stolen. This is evidence that could be used in court."

"Look at this." Lillian pointed to an entry near the end of the journal.

"Harrison knows I've discovered the truth. He came to me last night, charming and apologetic, claimed it was all a misunderstanding. But his eyes were cold. He said that sometimes people who dig too deeply find things they wish they hadn't, and that he'd hate for anything unfortunate to happen to me."

"That's a clear threat," Blackwood said.

The next entry was dated the day before Charlotte's death.

"I've written everything down and hidden this

journal where no one will find it. Katherine will know what to do if something happens to me. Harrison and his associates have stolen from dozens of families—perhaps hundreds. They've destroyed lives, and they've done it all while hiding behind respectability and social position. Someone has to stop them, even if that someone is just a society girl who asked too many questions."

The final entry was brief, written in a shakier hand:

"Harrison has asked me to meet him tonight at the house. He says he wants to explain everything, to make amends. I don't believe him, but I'm going anyway. If this is the end, at least I'll die knowing the truth is documented somewhere. Tell Katherine I love her. Tell her not to stop asking questions just because it's dangerous."

Lillian felt tears sting her eyes as she read Charlotte's final words. This young woman had known she was walking into danger but had gone anyway, trusting that her sister would ensure the truth eventually emerged.

"She was murdered that night," Lillian said quietly. "Harrison lured her to the house, killed her, and staged the suicide."

"But why the mourning dress?" Blackwood puzzled. "Why that specific detail?"

"To make the suicide look more plausible," Lillian theorized. "A woman mourning a broken engagement, so distraught she's already wearing mourning clothes. It adds drama to the narrative, makes the suicide seem more inevitable."

"And reinforces the idea that Charlotte was emotionally unstable." Blackwood began pacing the preparation room, his mind clearly working through possibilities. "The problem is that while this journal is compelling evidence of Harrison's motive, it doesn't prove he killed her. Everything here is circumstantial."

"Then we need to find direct evidence." Lillian closed the journal carefully. "The dress is our best lead. If we can prove Harrison purchased mourning attire before Charlotte died, it demonstrates premeditation."

"Madame Celeste's or Madame Colette's," Blackwood recalled. "Katherine wasn't certain of the name."

"We'll check both. And we'll need to do it carefully, if Harrison learns we're tracing his purchases, he'll destroy any records." Lillian rubbed her temples, feeling the late hour catching up with her. "We also need to warn the federal investigators about Charlotte's evidence. If they're already building a case against Harrison and his associates…"

"This journal could be the key to exposing the entire conspiracy." Blackwood stopped pacing and turned to face her. "Lillian, you realize what we're holding? This isn't just evidence of murder—it's documentation of years of fraud, theft, and exploitation. If we expose this…"

"We destroy some of Manhattan's most prominent families," Lillian finished. "Families with enough power and resources to make us disappear just as efficiently as they made Charlotte disappear."

"And you're still willing to pursue this investigation?"

Lillian looked around the preparation room where she'd spent so many years studying death, learning to read the stories written in flesh and bone. Charlotte Vandermeer's body had told a story of murder, just as the bodies of Mrs. Ashworth and countless others had told stories that the powerful preferred to silence.

"Charlotte Vandermeer died pursuing the truth," she said finally. "The least we can do is ensure her death wasn't meaningless."

"Then we continue." Blackwood's expression was grim but determined. "Tomorrow, we trace the dress. We build the case piece by piece until we have enough evidence that not even Fifth Avenue society can ignore it."

A sound from upstairs made them both freeze, footsteps on the floor above, moving toward the basement stairs. Lillian's father appeared at the top of the staircase, lamp in hand, his nightshirt hastily covered with a robe.

"Lillian? What are you doing here at this hour?" Edmund Cross descended the stairs slowly, his expression more confused than angry. "And Detective Blackwood? Has something happened?"

"We're working on a case, Father." Lillian moved to intercept him, not wanting him to see Charlotte's journal spread across the worktable. "We needed somewhere private to examine evidence."

Edmund's gaze swept the preparation room, taking in the open journal, their obvious agitation, and the late hour. "This is about the Vandermeer girl's death, isn't it? The one they're calling suicide."

"Father—"

"I heard about it. The whole city has heard about it." Edmund set his lamp on a shelf and studied his daughter with the particular intensity of a parent who'd learned to read his child's secrets. "You think she was murdered."

It wasn't a question. Lillian nodded slowly. "We have evidence that suggests she was killed because she discovered criminal activity among Manhattan's elite."

"Dangerous evidence, I assume, given the hour and the secrecy." Edmund moved to the worktable and glanced at the journal, though he didn't touch it. "Lillian, you're investigating people with considerable power and resources. People who've already killed once to protect their secrets."

"I know, Father."

"And you're going to continue anyway."

Again, not a question. Lillian met her father's eyes, seeing worry but also something else, perhaps pride, perhaps resignation. "Charlotte Vandermeer deserves justice."

Edmund was quiet for a long moment, then nodded slowly. "Very well. But you'll work carefully, and you'll keep me informed of any threats." He looked at Blackwood. "And you, Detective, will ensure my daughter doesn't take unnecessary risks."

"I'll do my best, sir," Blackwood replied respectfully.

"Your best had better be sufficient." Edmund's tone carried the weight of paternal authority. "I've already lost my wife. I won't lose my daughter to someone else's greed and corruption."

As Edmund returned upstairs, leaving them to their investigation, Lillian felt a surge of gratitude for her father's quiet support. He might not understand her need to pursue justice at any cost, but he accepted it and would protect her as much as his position allowed.

"We should get some rest," Blackwood said, checking his pocket watch. "A few hours at least. Tomorrow we'll need to be sharp if we're going to outwit Fifth Avenue's most dangerous criminals."

Lillian nodded, carefully securing Charlotte's journal in her medical bag. Tomorrow they would trace the mourning dress, build their case, and begin the process of exposing a conspiracy that reached into Manhattan's highest circles.

Charlotte had died asking questions. Now it was Lillian's turn to demand answers, whatever the cost.

Morning light filtered through the windows of Cross & Associates' office as Lillian studied the list Mrs. Duval had compiled overnight. True to her word, the society matron had identified three dressmakers on Madison Avenue whose names could fit Katherine's uncertain recollection: Madame Celeste's House of Mourning, Madame Colette's Fine Attire, and Madame Celestine's Boutique.

"Three shops, three slightly different names," Detective Blackwood observed, reading over her shoulder. "Any one of them could be the right place."

"Then we visit all three." Lillian checked her pocket watch, just past nine o'clock. "Dress shops open early to catch society matrons before their afternoon social calls."

"And how exactly do we ask about a mourning dress without alerting Harrison that we're investigating?" Blackwood's skepticism was evident. "If he learns we're tracing his purchases…"

"We don't ask about Harrison at all." Lillian pulled a

black dress from her wardrobe, one of the simpler mourning pieces she'd accumulated over years of funeral work. "Mrs. Duval will pose as a grieving widow seeking mourning attire. I'll accompany her as her companion. You'll wait outside and watch for anyone taking unusual interest in our visit."

"And what am I supposed to notice from the street?"

"Anyone who seems to be watching the shops. Anyone who follows us between locations." Lillian adjusted her hat in the small mirror above her desk. "If Harrison is as careful as Charlotte's journal suggests, he may have people monitoring the dressmakers to ensure no one asks uncomfortable questions."

Mrs. Duval arrived precisely at nine-thirty, dressed in elegant but subdued black that marked her as either recently bereaved or very fashion-conscious. She carried herself with the particular air of tragedy that wealthy widows cultivated when they wanted attention without appearing to seek it.

"You look perfect," Lillian told her. "Grieving but composed."

"I've had practice." Mrs. Duval's smile held old pain. "My husband's funeral taught me how to perform sorrow for society's benefit. Now, shall we see if we can purchase more than just grief at these establishments?"

Their first stop was Madame Celeste's House of Mourning, a narrow shop wedged between a milliner and a jeweler. The window display showed tasteful black crepe and silk, with discreet signs advertising "Complete Mourning Wardrobes for Discerning Families."

Inside, the shop was hushed and dimly lit, as if even the air itself was in mourning. A middle-aged woman in severe black approached them with practiced sympathy.

"Good morning. I am Madame Celeste. How may I assist you in this difficult time?"

Mrs. Duval's performance was flawless, a slight catch in her voice, a delicate dabbing at dry eyes with a black handkerchief. "My husband passed quite suddenly. I find myself in need of appropriate attire."

"Of course, of course. Please, sit." Madame Celeste guided them to velvet chairs while a younger assistant brought tea that neither woman touched. "When did your loss occur?"

"Three weeks ago." Mrs. Duval's timing was perfect, recent enough to explain the urgency, long enough that she wasn't expected to be completely devastated.

As Madame Celeste began showing various mourning dresses, Lillian studied the shop carefully. The walls were lined with cubbies containing folded garments, and a curtained doorway led to what she assumed was a back workroom. Near the counter, she spotted a large leather-bound ledger, likely the shop's order book.

"This is beautiful work," Mrs. Duval commented, examining a particularly elaborate black silk dress. "Do you create everything here, or do you also provide ready-made attire?"

"We do both, madam. Custom orders for those who have time, and a selection of ready-made garments for more immediate needs." Madame Celeste's tone carried just a hint of judgment, proper society ladies planned their mourning wardrobes in advance, not in the panicked aftermath of death.

"And gentlemen?" Lillian interjected casually. "Do you also serve male clients purchasing mourning attire for female relatives?"

Madame Celeste's expression flickered with surprise. "On occasion, yes, though it's somewhat unusual. Most families prefer that ladies handle such… delicate… matters themselves."

"Of course." Lillian smiled apologetically. "I only ask because a friend mentioned that her brother had purchased mourning clothes here as a gift. I thought it such a thoughtful gesture."

"Perhaps at one of the other establishments?" Madame Celeste's response was smooth but definitive. "I don't recall serving any gentlemen in the past several months."

They purchased a simple black shawl, Mrs. Duval insisted on leaving with something to avoid suspicion, and departed with polite thanks and promises to return.

"She was lying," Mrs. Duval said once they were

back on the street where Blackwood waited. "Did you see how her expression changed when you mentioned gentlemen customers?"

"I did." Lillian scanned the street, noting a man in a gray coat who seemed to be paying unusual attention to their group. "But whether she was lying about Harrison specifically or simply about serving male clients in general, I can't say."

"Two more shops to try." Blackwood fell into step beside them, his hand resting casually near his coat pocket. "And we have company, gray coat, across the street. He's been there since you entered the shop."

"I saw him." Lillian resisted the urge to look directly at the man. "Let's continue as planned. If he follows us to the next location, we'll know Harrison is having the shops watched."

Madame Colette's Fine Attire was several blocks south, occupying the ground floor of a more substantial building. Unlike Madame Celeste's somber establishment, this shop catered to a broader clientele—mourning attire, certainly, but also everyday dresses, evening gowns, and accessories.

The proprietress was younger than Lillian had expected, perhaps thirty, with sharp eyes that assessed them immediately as they entered.

"Good morning. How may I help you?"

Mrs. Duval repeated her performance, though with slight variations to keep it fresh. Madame Colette listened with professional sympathy while pulling mourning dresses from various displays.

"Your husband's name?" Madame Colette asked, producing a ledger from beneath the counter. "I like to make note of my clients and their circumstances. It helps me remember their needs for future visits."

"Mr. Edward Chambers," Mrs. Duval replied without hesitation, using a name she'd prepared in advance.

Madame Colette wrote it down carefully, then began showing various garments. As she worked, Lillian noticed something interesting, the proprietress kept glancing toward the front window, as if watching for someone.

"Have you been in business long?" Lillian asked, attempting to seem conversational rather than investigative.

"Five years this November. Long enough to serve many of Manhattan's finest families in their times of sorrow." Madame Colette's pride was evident. "I've dressed widows, daughters, even young gentlemen seeking appropriate mourning attire for unexpected losses."

"Gentlemen?" Lillian kept her tone casual. "That must be unusual."

"More common than you'd think. Sometimes a man loses a mother or sister suddenly and needs to outfit female relatives who are too distraught to shop." Madame Colette pulled out a particularly elegant black dress. "I had one such gentleman just last month—purchasing mourning attire for a young lady whose engagement had ended tragically. Such a thoughtful fiancé, ensuring she had proper clothing for her grief."

Lillian's pulse quickened. "How considerate. Was she bereaved?"

"In a manner of speaking. I believe he mentioned something about a broken engagement being a kind of death." Madame Colette's expression suggested she found the metaphor somewhat overdramatic. "He was very specific about the style and size—clearly knew the lady well."

"Do you recall his name?" The question was too direct, too eager, but Lillian couldn't help herself.

Madame Colette's eyes narrowed slightly. "Why do you ask?"

"My friend's brother," Lillian improvised quickly. "She mentioned he'd purchased mourning attire as a gift, and I thought it might have been here."

"Ah." Madame Colette's suspicion didn't entirely fade, but she consulted her ledger. "The gentleman's name was… let me see… Mr. H. Ashford. Quite generous, actually, paid in cash and didn't quibble over the price."

There it was. Direct evidence linking Harrison to the purchase of mourning attire before Charlotte's death. Lillian forced herself to remain calm, though her mind was racing.

"How lovely," she managed. "And when was this purchase?"

"Early September, I believe. Yes, here it is—September eighth." Madame Colette looked up from her ledger. "Why such interest in another client's purchases?"

"Simple curiosity," Mrs. Duval interjected smoothly, sensing Lillian's excitement might give them away. "My companion is writing a book about modern mourning customs. She finds these personal touches so fascinating."

"A book?" Madame Colette's suspicion returned full force. "What sort of book?"

Before they could answer, the shop door opened and a man entered—not the gray coat from earlier, but someone else. Well-dressed, perhaps forty, with the confident bearing of someone accustomed to authority. His eyes swept the shop before settling on Lillian and Mrs. Duval with uncomfortable intensity.

"Madame Colette," he said pleasantly, though his smile didn't reach his eyes. "I hope I'm not interrupting."

"Mr. Thornton! What a surprise." Madame Colette's nervousness was obvious. "I wasn't expecting you until this afternoon."

Thornton. Robert Thornton, one of Harrison's associates mentioned in Charlotte's journal. Lillian felt ice in her veins as the man approached.

"I happened to be in the neighborhood and thought I'd check on those alterations we discussed." His attention remained fixed on Lillian and Mrs. Duval. "And who are these charming ladies?"

"Mrs. Chambers and her companion," Madame Colette supplied, her discomfort growing. "They were just inquiring about mourning attire."

"How tragic." Thornton's smile widened. "Recent loss?"

"My husband, three weeks ago." Mrs. Duval maintained her performance admirably.

"My condolences. And your companion, you mentioned she was writing a book?" Thornton stepped closer, close enough that Lillian could smell his expensive cologne. "About mourning customs, was it?"

"That's correct." Lillian met his eyes steadily, refusing to show the fear creeping up her spine.

"Fascinating. I've always been interested in how society handles death." His tone was conversational, but there was threat beneath it. "All the rituals and traditions designed to make the uncomfortable more… manageable. Though sometimes, I think we spend too much time questioning what should simply be accepted."

The warning was clear. Lillian glanced toward the door, where she could see Blackwood outside, though he was facing away and hadn't noticed Thornton's arrival.

"We should be going," Mrs. Duval said, gathering her things. "Madame Colette, thank you for your time. I'll return when I've had a chance to consider my options."

"Of course." Madame Colette's relief was palpable. "Please do."

As they moved toward the door, Thornton stepped into their path, not blocking them entirely, but making it clear they would have to brush past him to leave.

"Before you go," he said pleasantly, "might I ask which publisher is producing your book on mourning customs? I have friends in the publishing industry who might be interested."

"We're still seeking the right publisher," Lillian replied, edging toward the door. "If you'll excuse us—"

"And where might I find your office, should my friends wish to contact you?"

"That won't be necessary." Mrs. Duval's voice carried steel beneath its polite surface. "Now, if you'll kindly let us pass."

For a moment, Thornton didn't move, and Lillian thought he might actually prevent them from leaving. But then he stepped aside with an exaggerated bow.

"Of course. Do forgive my curiosity. I hope your book finds great success." His eyes locked with Lillian's. "Though I should warn you, some subjects are better left unexamined. Digging into other people's grief can be… dangerous… for those doing the digging."

They escaped to the street, where Blackwood immediately noticed their agitation. "What happened?"

"Robert Thornton," Lillian said quietly as they walked quickly away from the shop. "One of Harrison's associates. He was at the dress shop, and he knows we were asking questions."

"Did you get what you needed before he arrived?"

"Yes." Mrs. Duval's composure was cracking slightly, her hands trembling. "Madame Colette confirmed that Harrison purchased mourning attire on September eighth, weeks before Charlotte's death."

"That's premeditation," Blackwood said grimly. "He planned her murder well in advance."

"And now his associates know we're investigating." Lillian glanced back toward the shop, where she could see Thornton standing in the window, watching them. "We need to move quickly. If they realize how much evidence we have…"

"They'll destroy records, threaten witnesses, possibly worse." Blackwood guided them toward a waiting carriage. "We need to get that ledger entry documented officially before Madame Colette destroys it, or before Thornton destroys it for her."

As they climbed into the carriage, Lillian felt the weight of what they'd uncovered. Harrison had purchased mourning clothes weeks before Charlotte's death, proving he'd planned to stage her suicide long before the actual murder. Combined with Charlotte's journal documenting his threats and the fraud conspiracy, they had a case that could destroy him and his associates.

But they also now had enemies who knew they were investigating, enemies with resources and ruthlessness. The gray coat following them, Thornton's convenient appearance at the dress shop, these weren't coincidences. They were warnings.

The race was on to build their case before Harrison and his associates could silence them the same way they'd silenced Charlotte.

"We need to contact the federal investigators," Lillian said as the carriage pulled into traffic. "Today. Before Thornton has time to warn Harrison that we've connected him to the dress purchase."

"Agreed." Blackwood's expression was grim. "But we also need to warn Katherine. If Harrison realizes we have

Charlotte's journal and evidence of premeditation…"

"He'll know Katherine gave us the evidence." Mrs. Duval's face had gone pale. "She's in terrible danger."

As Manhattan rushed past the carriage windows, Lillian realized they'd crossed a threshold. No more careful investigation and discreet inquiries. They were in open conflict now with some of the city's most powerful and dangerous men.

Charlotte had died pursuing the truth. Now it was a race to ensure that truth saw the light before anyone else had to die for it.

The carriage had barely stopped at Cross & Associates when Lillian leaped out, already moving toward the building's entrance. Detective Blackwood and Mrs. Duval followed close behind, all three understanding the urgency without needing to discuss it further.

"We split up," Lillian said as they climbed the stairs to the office. "Detective Blackwood, you contact the federal investigators. Tell them we have evidence of systematic fraud and a murder committed to cover it up. Mrs. Duval, can you—"

"I'll go to Katherine immediately," Mrs. Duval interrupted, already gathering her things. "If Harrison suspects she gave us the journal, he won't wait for subtlety. I'll take her to my boarding house whether her parents approve or not."

"They'll call the police," Blackwood warned.

"Theodore Vandermeer has enough connections to have you arrested for kidnapping."

"Then you'd better ensure the federal investigators are ready to intervene before that happens." Mrs. Duval's determination was absolute. "I won't let that girl die while we're building a case."

She was gone before either could argue further, leaving Lillian and Blackwood alone in the office. Through the window, they could see Mrs. Duval's carriage already pulling away toward Fifth Avenue.

"The federal investigators," Blackwood said, checking his pocket watch. "I have a contact in the Treasury Department—someone who helped during the Whitmore investigation. He's discreet and won't alert anyone we don't trust."

"How long will it take?"

"An hour to reach him, perhaps another hour to convince him to act immediately rather than through official channels." Blackwood was already gathering Charlotte's journal and the notes they'd compiled. "We need leverage—something that makes them move now rather than tomorrow."

Lillian pulled out the ledger page she'd carefully copied while Madame Colette had been distracted by Mrs. Duval's questions. "The dress purchase. September eighth, paid in cash, specific measurements matching Charlotte's size. Combined with Charlotte's journal documenting Harrison's threats and the fraud conspiracy—"

"It's enough." Blackwood studied the evidence with professional assessment. "Not enough to convict in court yet, but enough to justify federal intervention. Especially if we can demonstrate Katherine is in immediate danger."

A knock at the door made them both freeze. Too soon for Mrs. Duval to return, and their legitimate clients knew to send telegrams before visiting. Lillian moved toward her desk where she kept a small derringer—a gift from Mrs. Duval after the Whitmore affair. She'd never seriously expected to need it.

"Who is it?" Blackwood called, his hand on his revolver.

"Telegram for Miss Cross. Urgent delivery."

They exchanged glances. Blackwood approached the door carefully, opening it just enough to see a young messenger boy holding an envelope.

"Who sent it?"

"Don't know, sir. Just paid to deliver it quick-like." The boy thrust the envelope forward and disappeared down the stairs before either could question him further.

Lillian opened the envelope with trembling fingers. The telegram was brief and devastating:

*STOP INVESTIGATION IMMEDIATELY. KATHERINE VANDERMEER'S SAFETY DEPENDS ON YOUR COOPERATION. DESTROY ALL EVIDENCE. WE WILL CONTACT YOU WITH INSTRUCTIONS.*
*– A FRIEND*

"They have her." Lillian's voice was barely above a whisper. "Or they're planning to take her. Mrs. Duval is walking into a trap."

Blackwood was already moving toward the door. "We need to warn her before she reaches the Vandermeer mansion."

"There's no time. She left five minutes ago, she could already be there." Lillian grabbed her coat and medical bag, checking that the derringer was loaded. "We go after her. Now."

They clattered down the stairs and into the street, where Blackwood flagged down a cab with the authority of his police credentials.

"Fifth Avenue, Vandermeer mansion. As fast as

you can manage, and there's an extra dollar in it if you don't spare the horses."

The driver needed no further encouragement. They careened through Manhattan's midday traffic, dodging pedestrians and slower vehicles with reckless speed. Lillian clutched the side of the cab, her mind racing through worst-case scenarios.

"If they've already taken Katherine…" she began.

"Then we get her back." Blackwood's jaw was set with determination. "But first, we ensure Mrs. Duval doesn't become their second hostage."

The Vandermeer mansion appeared ahead, looking as imposing as ever in the afternoon light. But something was wrong, the front door stood open, and Lillian could see servants gathered in the entrance, their expressions carrying panic rather than the usual studied neutrality.

Mrs. Duval's carriage was stopped haphazardly near the entrance, the driver nowhere to be seen.

"Oh God," Lillian breathed.

They leaped from their cab before it fully stopped, running toward the mansion. A maid saw them approaching and burst into tears.

"She's gone! Miss Katherine is gone!"

"When?" Blackwood demanded, his detective instincts taking over. "When did she disappear?"

"This morning, sir. Mrs. Vandermeer went to wake her for breakfast, and her room was empty. Bed not slept in, window open…" The maid's words tumbled out in a rush of fear and gossip. "They're saying she ran away, but Miss Katherine would never—"

"Where is Mrs. Duval?" Lillian interrupted. "The woman who just arrived?"

"Inside with the family, miss. Mr. Vandermeer is, well, he's not pleased to have visitors just now."

Lillian and Blackwood pushed past the servants

into the mansion's grand entrance hall. Voices echoed from the parlor, Theodore Vandermeer's angry baritone, Mrs. Duval's calmer but insistent responses, and Mrs. Vandermeer's icy tones.

"—no right to come here making accusations!" Theodore was saying as they entered the parlor.

The scene was chaos barely contained by social propriety. Theodore Vandermeer stood near the fireplace, his face red with anger. Mrs. Vandermeer sat in a chair by the window, her composure cracked but not entirely shattered. Mrs. Duval faced them both, still wearing her mourning attire from the dress shop investigation.

"I'm not making accusations," Mrs. Duval said firmly. "I'm stating facts. Your daughter's life is in danger—"

"My daughter has run away because she couldn't accept her sister's suicide," Theodore interrupted. "This is a family matter, Mrs. Duval, and not your concern."

"She didn't run away." Lillian stepped into the parlor, ignoring the shocked expressions her interruption created. "Katherine was taken, or she fled because she knew she was in danger. Either way, she's not safe."

"Miss Cross." Mrs. Vandermeer's voice could have frozen water. "You are not welcome in this house."

"I don't care about your welcome. I care about Katherine's life." Lillian pulled out the telegram. "We received this thirty minutes ago. It's a threat, stop investigating or Katherine suffers."

Theodore snatched the telegram from her hands, his anger shifting to something closer to fear as he read it. "This is… who sent this?"

"The same people who killed Charlotte," Blackwood said quietly. "Harrison Ashford and his associates."

"That's absurd." But Theodore's protest lacked

conviction. "Harrison is Charlotte's fiancé, was her fiancé. He had no reason to harm her."

"Except that Charlotte discovered he was running a massive fraud scheme targeting immigrant families," Lillian countered. "She documented everything in a journal that Katherine gave us last night. Harrison bought mourning attire weeks before Charlotte died, planning to stage her suicide. When Charlotte threatened to expose him and his associates, he killed her."

The silence that followed was profound. Mrs. Vandermeer's composure finally cracked completely, tears streaming down her face. Theodore sank into a chair as if his legs could no longer support him.

"Charlotte was investigating Harrison?" he asked, his voice hollow.

"She discovered that he and several other wealthy young men, Robert Thornton, William Hartley, Charles Pemberton, were systematically defrauding immigrant investors. Hundreds of thousands of dollars stolen over three years." Lillian softened her tone slightly, seeing genuine shock rather than complicity in Theodore's face. "She was going to expose them. They couldn't allow that."

"And Katherine?" Mrs. Vandermeer asked through her tears. "What do they want with Katherine?"

"The journal. Evidence of their crimes." Blackwood moved to the window, scanning the street outside. "They know we have it, and they're using Katherine as leverage to force us to destroy it."

"Then destroy it!" Theodore's anguish was raw. "Give them whatever they want. I've already lost one daughter, I won't lose both."

"If we destroy the evidence, Katherine becomes the only remaining witness to their crimes," Lillian explained gently. "They'll kill her anyway to ensure their safety. The only way to save her is to expose them so completely that harming her becomes pointless."

"That's a gamble with my daughter's life."

"It's the only gamble that gives her a chance." Mrs. Duval moved to sit beside Mrs. Vandermeer, taking the other woman's hand in a gesture of solidarity. "These men have already killed once. They'll kill again without hesitation. The only thing that can stop them is the threat of complete exposure."

A commotion from the entrance hall interrupted them, raised voices, the sound of a struggle. Moments later, a young footman burst into the parlor.

"Sir! There's a gentleman demanding entrance. Says he has a message from Miss Katherine's captors."

"Send him in," Theodore commanded.

The man who entered was neither Harrison nor any of his known associates, just an ordinary-looking individual in modest clothing who could have been anyone. He carried an envelope with obvious nervousness.

"Mr. Vandermeer? I was paid to deliver this. Told to wait for your response." He thrust the envelope toward Theodore with trembling hands.

Theodore opened it with shaking fingers and read aloud: "We have Katherine. She is unharmed but will remain so only if you cooperate. Miss Cross and Detective Blackwood will bring Charlotte's journal and all related evidence to the Union Club at six o'clock this evening. Come alone. Any attempt to involve authorities will result in Katherine's immediate death. Further instructions will be provided at the club."

The messenger fidgeted. "I'm to bring back your answer, sir. Will you comply?"

"Yes," Theodore said immediately. "Tell them yes."

"Mr. Vandermeer—" Blackwood began.

"Tell them yes!" Theodore's voice broke. "Whatever they want. Just bring my daughter home safely."

The messenger nodded and fled, clearly relieved to be away from the raw emotion filling the parlor.

"This is a trap," Blackwood said once the man was gone. "They'll take the evidence and kill both Katherine and anyone who delivers it."

"I know." Lillian's mind was already working through possibilities. "But it also gives us something valuable—time and a location. The Union Club at six o'clock. Four hours to prepare."

"Prepare how?" Theodore demanded. "They've forbidden authorities—"

"They've forbidden obvious authorities." Lillian turned to Blackwood. "But federal investigators conducting surveillance on a suspected criminal conspiracy? That's different from uniformed police responding to a hostage situation."

Understanding dawned in Blackwood's eyes. "If we can get the Treasury agents to the Union Club before six o'clock, set up positions around the building."

"We walk in with the evidence as demanded, they'll either produce Katherine or reveal where she's being held, and federal agents can intervene before anyone gets killed." Lillian looked at Theodore. "But we need you to trust us. No interference, no private security, no attempts to negotiate separately."

"And if your plan fails?" Mrs. Vandermeer's voice was small, frightened. "If my daughter dies because you insisted on involving authorities?"

"Then she dies anyway," Mrs. Duval said bluntly. "These men are murderers. They won't release Katherine even if you give them everything they demand. Miss Cross and Detective Blackwood are offering the only chance your daughter has."

Theodore and his wife exchanged long looks, communicating in the silent language of parents facing impossible choices.

"What do you need from us?" Theodore asked finally.

"Everything you know about the Union Club," Blackwood said. "Layout, membership, staff, anything that might help federal agents position themselves effectively."

"And stay here," Lillian added. "Wait for our contact. When this is over, you'll either get Katherine back safely, or…" She couldn't finish the sentence.

"Or we'll at least know who to bury alongside Charlotte," Mrs. Vandermeer said quietly.

As they prepared to leave, gathering the information they needed and planning their approach, Lillian felt the weight of what they were attempting. This wasn't a careful investigation anymore—it was a rescue operation with Katherine's life hanging in the balance and powerful men desperate to protect their secrets.

Charlotte had died pursuing the truth. Now Katherine's life depended on that truth being exposed completely and immediately.

Four hours until the exchange. Four hours to save a life and expose a conspiracy.

It would have to be enough.

The Treasury Department office was tucked away in a nondescript building near City Hall, far from the marble grandeur of other federal facilities. Detective Blackwood led Lillian through corridors that smelled of paper, ink, and the particular mustiness of bureaucracy conducted in cramped quarters.

"Special Agent Loomis," Blackwood said to a middle-aged man bent over a desk covered with financial documents. "We need your help. Urgently."

Agent Loomis looked up with the weary expression of someone accustomed to urgent requests that rarely proved truly urgent. But his eyes sharpened when he saw Charlotte's journal and the evidence Lillian spread across his desk.

"This is about the Vandermeer case," he said, not a question. "Word's already reached us that you've been asking uncomfortable questions in uncomfortable places."

"How did you—" Lillian began.

"We've had our own investigation running for six months. Stock fraud targeting immigrant communities, money laundering through legitimate businesses, possible connections to several suspicious deaths." Loomis's finger traced across their evidence. "Harrison Ashford and his associates are at the center of it all. But we've been unable to gather enough evidence for indictments."

"Until now." Blackwood tapped Charlotte's journal. "Charlotte Vandermeer documented everything, names, dates, amounts stolen, specific victims. And we can prove Harrison murdered her to prevent this information from becoming public."

Loomis read through Charlotte's journal with increasing intensity, occasionally making notes in his own ledger. When he reached the final entries, Charlotte's documentation of Harrison's threats and her knowledge that she was in danger, his jaw tightened.

"This girl knew she was walking into death," he said quietly.

"She believed the truth was worth the risk." Lillian pulled out the threatening telegram. "Now her sister has been kidnapped. They're demanding we bring all evidence to the Union Club at six o'clock in exchange for Katherine's safe return."

"It's a trap."

"Obviously. Which is why we need federal agents positioned around the club before we arrive." Blackwood consulted the notes Theodore Vandermeer had provided. "The Union Club occupies four floors—main entrance on Fifth Avenue, service entrance on the side street, and a private members' entrance in the rear."

Loomis stood and moved to a map of Manhattan pinned to his wall. "The club is in the heart of Fifth

Avenue society. Any obvious federal presence will be noticed immediately."

"Then be less obvious." Lillian joined him at the map. " Deliverymen, street vendors, maintenance workers, anything that gives your agents clear sight lines without arousing suspicion."

"You're talking about a significant operation with less than" Morrison checked his pocket watch, "three hours to prepare. I'll need approval from my superiors, coordination with local police—"

"There's no time for proper channels," Blackwood interrupted. "By the time you navigate bureaucracy, Katherine Vandermeer will be dead and every piece of evidence will be destroyed."

"Then you're asking me to risk my career, possibly face dismissal, on the strength of a dead girl's journal and your assurances that this isn't some elaborate society drama."Loomis's tone wasn't hostile, just realistic. "Give me one reason why I should stake everything on your investigation."

Lillian met his eyes steadily. "Because if you don't, Harrison Ashford and his associates will have murdered two young women and stolen hundreds of thousands of dollars from the city's most vulnerable residents, and they'll continue operating because people like you waited for proper channels instead of acting on evidence."

The silence stretched until Lillian thought she'd miscalculated, pushed too hard against a man whose authority she needed. But then Loomis smiled grimly.

"My mother was Irish," he said quietly. "Came to this city with nothing, worked herself to exhaustion in factories, died before she could see me make something of myself. I became a federal agent to protect people like her from men like Harrison Ashford." He turned back to his desk and began pulling out files. "I'll give you your operation, Miss Cross. But if this goes wrong, we all hang together."

The next two hours were a blur of activity. Morrison assembled a team of six trusted agents, all men who'd worked immigrant fraud cases and had personal stakes in seeing justice done. They studied the Union Club's layout, planned positioning, discussed contingencies for various scenarios.

"We can't enter the club without invitation," Loomis explained as they finalized their approach. "It's private property, members only. Even with federal authority, bursting in without clear evidence of a crime in progress could invalidate any arrests."

"Then we provide evidence of a crime in progress," Lillian said. "When they take the journal from us, they're accepting stolen property. When they threaten us regarding Katherine, they're admitting to kidnapping. Let them incriminate themselves, then you have cause to intervene."

"Assuming they're stupid enough to confess in front of witnesses."

"They're arrogant enough to believe they're untouchable," Blackwood countered. "That's different from stupid, but it serves the same purpose."

At five-thirty, they gathered for final preparations. Loomis's agents departed in pairs, each taking assigned positions around the Union Club. Two would pose as newspaper vendors on opposite corners. Two would occupy a building across the street with clear sight lines to the club's entrance. The final two would position themselves near the service entrance, ready to move if Katherine was being held in the building.

"What about us?" Lillian asked, adjusting the derringer concealed in her coat pocket.

"You walk in exactly as demanded," Loomis said. "Bring the journal, appear cooperative. Our agents will be watching, if anything goes wrong, they'll intervene within seconds."

"And if Katherine isn't at the club?" The question had been haunting Lillian since they'd received the ransom demand. "If they're holding her elsewhere and this is just a trap to eliminate us and recover the evidence?"

"Then we'll have Harrison and his associates in custody and we'll make them tell us where she is." Loomis's confidence sounded forced. "One way or another, Miss Cross, this ends tonight."

Mrs. Duval arrived at five-forty-five, having spent the intervening hours at the Vandermeer mansion providing what comfort she could to Charlotte's distraught parents.

"Theodore wanted to come," she reported. "I had to physically restrain him from following you to the club. He's convinced Katherine will die and he should be there."

"He's not wrong about the danger," Blackwood observed.

"Which is why we're here instead of him." Mrs. Duval's composure was back in place, though Lillian could see the fear beneath it. "What do you need from me?"

"Stay outside with Loomis's command post," Lillian said. "If anything goes wrong—"

"If anything goes wrong, I'm coming in after you." Mrs. Duval's tone brooked no argument. "You've become rather important to me, my dear. I have no intention of losing you to Harrison Ashford's desperation."

At five minutes to six, Lillian and Blackwood approached the Union Club's imposing entrance. The building was a monument to masculine privilege—dark stone, heavy doors, and an air of exclusivity that made clear women were tolerated only as guests, never as equals.

A doorman in elaborate livery stopped them at the entrance.

"Members only, sir, madam."

"We're expected," Blackwood said, producing a card that Loomis had provided—some sort of federal credential that looked official without actually identifying him as a detective. "Mr. Ashford is expecting us."

The doorman's expression suggested he found their presence irregular but not sufficient cause for refusal. He stepped aside, allowing them entry into a world of leather, mahogany, and cigar smoke.

The interior was everything Lillian had imagined, ornate furnishings, oil paintings of distinguished gentlemen, an atmosphere of self-satisfied power. A few members glanced at them with mild curiosity before returning to their newspapers and quiet conversations.

A servant approached immediately. "Mr. Ashford is waiting in the library. Follow me."

They were led through corridors lined with books and portraits, past rooms where elderly men dozed in chairs and younger men discussed business over brandy. The library was on the third floor, accessible by a narrow staircase that made Lillian acutely aware of how trapped they'd be if things went badly.

Harrison Ashford stood by a window overlooking Fifth Avenue, his back to them as they entered. He wasn't alone, Robert Thornton occupied a leather chair near the fireplace, and another man Lillian recognized from Charlotte's journal as William Hartley leaned against a bookshelf with studied casualness.

"Miss Cross, Detective Blackwood." Harrison turned, and Lillian was struck by how normal he looked, handsome, well-groomed, every inch the respectable society gentleman. There was nothing in his appearance to suggest he was a murderer and fraud. "Thank you for being punctual."

"Where is Katherine?" Lillian demanded, not bothering with pleasantries.

"Safe, for the moment." Harrison gestured to chairs that neither Lillian nor Blackwood accepted. "Did you bring what we requested?"

Lillian held up Charlotte's journal. "Evidence of systematic fraud, documentation of threats, and proof that you purchased mourning attire weeks before Charlotte's death. Everything needed to see you hanged for murder."

"Such dramatic language." Thornton's smile was cold. "You should be careful about making accusations you can't prove."

"I *can* prove everything." Lillian opened the journal to Charlotte's final entries. "She documented your threats, Harrison. She knew you were planning to kill her, and she wrote it all down."

"Charlotte was emotionally unstable," Harrison said smoothly. "Everyone knows that. Her journal is the fantasy of a troubled woman, nothing more."

"Then why kidnap her sister? Why go to such elaborate lengths to recover a book of fantasies?"

Harrison's composure flickered slightly. "We haven't kidnapped anyone. Katherine ran away because she couldn't accept her sister's suicide. Any suggestion otherwise is pure speculation."

"Is it?" Blackwood stepped forward. "Then you won't mind if we search this building for her. Just to confirm she's not being held here against her will."

"This is a private club, Detective. You have no authority here." Hartley's voice carried threat. "Give us the journal and leave quietly. That's your only option."

"Actually," Loomis's voice came from the doorway, "they have several options. As do I."

The federal agent stood in the entrance flanked by two of his men, all three with weapons drawn.

Behind them, Lillian could see more agents filing up the stairs.

"Special Agent Loomis, Treasury Department." He produced his credentials. "Harrison Ashford, Robert Thornton, William Hartley, you're all under arrest for conspiracy to commit fraud, money laundering, and suspicion of murder."

Harrison's face went white. "You have no authority—"

"I have federal authority, which supersedes your club membership considerably." Loomis nodded to his agents. "Secure them."

What happened next occurred so quickly that Lillian barely processed it. Thornton lunged for a side door, but Loomis's agents blocked his escape. Hartley reached for something in his coat—a weapon, Lillian realized, but Blackwood was faster, pinning the man's arm before he could draw.

Only Harrison remained still, his expression shifting from shock to cold calculation.

"Where is Katherine Vandermeer?" Loomis demanded.

"I have no idea what you're talking about."

"The ransom demand. The kidnapping. Where is she?"

Harrison's smile was terrible in its calm confidence. "Prove I sent any ransom demand. Prove I've kidnapped anyone. You have nothing but speculation and the fantasies written by a mentally unstable woman."

Lillian felt cold realization wash over her. Harrison had been careful, so careful. The telegram had been unsigned. The ransom demand had been delivered by a paid messenger who likely couldn't identify who'd hired him. Even Charlotte's journal, damning as it was, contained no direct confession of murder—just threats that could be interpreted as concern rather than malice.

"We have the dress purchase," she said desperately. "You bought mourning attire weeks before Charlotte died. That proves premeditation."

"It proves I purchased a gift for someone. Not a crime." Harrison's confidence was growing. "You have no bodies showing signs of murder—Charlotte's death was officially ruled suicide. You have no witnesses to any crime. You have nothing except the paranoid writings of a girl who couldn't accept her engagement ending."

"And Katherine?" Loomis pressed. "If you haven't kidnapped her, where is she?"

"How should I know? Perhaps she's at the Vandermeer estate. Perhaps she's run away. Perhaps she's anywhere in Manhattan." Harrison spread his hands. "You can arrest me, Agent Loomis, but you'll have to release me within hours because you have no evidence of any actual crime."

The terrible thing was that he was right. Lillian could see it in Loomis's expression, in the way the federal agent's certainty wavered. Charlotte's journal was compelling but circumstantial. The dress purchase was suspicious but not proof of murder. Without Katherine's testimony or her physical presence as proof of kidnapping, they had nothing solid enough to hold these men.

"However," Harrison continued, his voice turning silky with threat, "if you do insist on this harassment, if you continue to spread lies about respectable businessmen, I imagine the consequences will be… unfortunate. For everyone involved."

"Is that a threat?" Blackwood demanded.

"It's a statement of fact. Reputations can be destroyed, careers can be ended, and accidents—well, accidents happen to people who make themselves nuisances." Harrison looked directly at Lillian. "Charlotte learned that lesson. I'd hate for others to follow her example."

Before anyone could respond, a commotion from downstairs drew their attention, shouting, the sound of something breaking, and then a girl's voice, sharp with fury and unmistakably alive.

"Get your hands off me! I'm Katherine Vandermeer and I demand to see a police officer!"

Everyone froze for a heartbeat, and then Loomis was moving, his agents following. They thundered down the stairs toward the source of the commotion, leaving Lillian and Blackwood to ensure Harrison and his associates didn't escape.

In the main entrance hall, they found Katherine Vandermeer, dirty, disheveled, but very much alive—being restrained by two club servants who clearly had no idea what to do with an irate society girl who'd apparently broken in through a back window.

"Katherine!" Lillian's relief was overwhelming.

"Miss Cross! Thank God!" Katherine struggled free of the confused servants and rushed toward them. "I've been hiding in the basement since they brought me here this morning. I heard voices upstairs and thought if I made enough noise—"

"You were here the whole time," Loomis said with dawning understanding. "In this building."

"They brought me in through the service entrance before dawn," Katherine confirmed, her words tumbling out in a rush. "Three men, all masked. They locked me in a storage room in the basement and told me I'd be released unharmed if my family cooperated. But I heard them talking, they were planning to kill me regardless, make it look like I'd run away and met with some accident."

"Who were these men?" Loomis demanded. "Can you identify them?"

"Not the ones who grabbed me from my room, they wore masks. But I heard voices I recognized."

Katherine's eyes found Harrison across the entrance hall. "Including yours, Harrison. You gave instructions to the men holding me. You told them to wait for the exchange and then eliminate me along with anyone who delivered the evidence."

Harrison's composure finally cracked completely. "That's absurd! She's hysterical, making up stories—"

"I heard you," Katherine said with absolute certainty. "You came to check on me around noon. You told the guards that once you had Charlotte's journal, I was a liability that needed to be eliminated. Those were your exact words, 'eliminated as efficiently as Charlotte was.'"

The confession hung in the air like smoke from a fired gun. Harrison realized too late what he'd walked into, how completely Katherine's testimony had destroyed his careful denials.

"You heard nothing," he tried weakly. "You're confused, traumatized—"

"I'm the daughter of Theodore Vandermeer and the sister of Charlotte Vandermeer," Katherine said with quiet fury. "And I'm the witness who will see you hanged for murder."

Loomis nodded to his agents. "Secure Mr. Ashford and his associates. The charges now include kidnapping, attempted murder, and conspiracy to commit murder."

As federal agents moved to arrest the three men, Lillian felt the tension that had been coiling inside her since Katherine's disappearance finally release. They'd done it. Against all odds, they'd saved Katherine and secured evidence that would destroy Harrison's conspiracy.

But as Harrison was led away in chains, his final look toward Lillian carried a promise that chilled her to the bone. This might be over for him, but there were others involved in the fraud conspiracy, other wealthy men whose fortunes depended on silence and cooperation.

The battle was won. But the war against corruption in Manhattan's highest circles had only just begun.

The Vandermeer mansion had never seemed so full of life as it did three days after Katherine's rescue. Lillian stood in the parlor that had once been the scene of tense confrontations, watching as Theodore Vandermeer embraced his daughter for perhaps the hundredth time since her return.

"I still can't believe she hid in that basement for hours," Mrs. Duval said quietly beside Lillian, sipping tea from one of the Vandermeer's finest porcelain cups. "The courage that must have required."

"She's her sister's sister," Lillian replied, using the phrase Mrs. Vandermeer had repeated like a mantra since Katherine's safe return. "Charlotte taught her that truth was worth fighting for, even when fighting seemed impossible."

The past three days had been a whirlwind of

activity. Harrison Ashford, Robert Thornton, and William Hartley remained in federal custody, facing charges of fraud, conspiracy, kidnapping, and murder. Special Agent Loomis's investigation had expanded rapidly once Charlotte's journal provided names and dates, already, two dozen immigrant families had come forward with stories of being swindled, and the Treasury Department estimated the full scope of the fraud exceeded half a million dollars.

"The newspapers are calling it the scandal of the decade," Detective Blackwood observed, joining them with his own cup of tea. He still looked uncomfortable in the Vandermeer's elegant parlor, though his discomfort had shifted from class consciousness to simple unfamiliarity with afternoon social calls. "Every society page is full of speculation about which other families might be involved."

"Good," Mrs. Vandermeer said firmly, approaching their group with surprising steadiness. In the days since Katherine's rescue, Charlotte's mother had transformed from a woman desperate to maintain appearances into someone focused entirely on justice for her murdered daughter. "Let them speculate. Let every family in Manhattan society look over their shoulders and wonder if their sons are next to be exposed."

Lillian had watched this transformation with professional interest. Grief, she'd learned in her years preparing bodies for burial, either destroyed people or revealed who they truly were beneath social masks. Mrs. Vandermeer, stripped of her pretensions by tragedy, had proven to be stronger than anyone had suspected.

"The trial will be difficult," Lillian warned gently. "Defense attorneys will try to paint Charlotte as unstable, will suggest Katherine's testimony is unreliable due to trauma."

"Let them try." Katherine's voice was steady as

she joined the conversation, having finally extracted herself from her father's protective embrace. "I heard Harrison confess. I heard him order my death. No attorney can argue away what I witnessed."

"They'll try regardless," Blackwood cautioned. "Harrison's family has significant resources, and they'll hire the best defense money can buy."

"Then we'll ensure the prosecution is better prepared." Theodore Vandermeer's voice carried new authority, not the bluster of wealth and position, but the determination of a father seeking justice for his murdered child. "I've already met with the district attorney. My testimony, combined with Katherine's, Charlotte's journal, and the physical evidence you've gathered, will be sufficient to convict."

"Your testimony?" Lillian was surprised. "What can you testify to?"

Theodore's expression grew troubled. "Harrison approached me six months ago about a business investment. He was quite persuasive, talked about opportunities in immigrant communities, guaranteed returns, minimal risk. I gave him fifty thousand dollars."

The room fell silent. Mrs. Vandermeer's hand went to her throat.

"Theodore," she breathed. "You never mentioned—"

"Because I was ashamed." Theodore's voice cracked slightly. "I gave money to the man who was defrauding vulnerable families, who murdered our daughter when she discovered his crimes. If I'd done proper due diligence, if I'd asked the right questions instead of being seduced by promises of easy profit…"

"You didn't know," Katherine said firmly, moving to her father's side. "Harrison fooled everyone, that was his talent. Looking respectable while being monstrous."

"Nevertheless." Theodore straightened his

shoulders. "I'll testify to his tactics, his persuasiveness, the way he targeted even wealthy investors who should have known better. If it helps convict him, then perhaps some good can come from my foolishness."

A soft knock at the parlor door interrupted them. The butler entered with an apologetic expression.

"Pardon the interruption, but there's a gentleman here to see Miss Cross and Detective Blackwood. A Mr. Alistair Penrose from The Manhattan Observer?"

Lillian and Blackwood exchanged glances. Penrose, the journalist who'd helped them during the Whitmore investigation, was exactly the kind of ally they needed to ensure the story received proper public attention.

"Show him in," Theodore said before either could respond. "If he's here about the case, he should hear everything."

Alistair Penrose entered with the slightly disheveled appearance of a man who'd been working frantically to meet deadlines. His notebook was already in hand, ink-stained fingers ready to record whatever information might be shared.

"Miss Cross, Detective Blackwood." He nodded respectfully to them before addressing the Vandermeers. "Mr. and Mrs. Vandermeer, Miss Vandermeer, I'm deeply sorry for your loss. But I'm also grateful for the opportunity to tell Charlotte's story properly. Too often, murdered women are reduced to scandalous headlines. Charlotte deserves better."

"What sort of story are you planning?" Mrs. Vandermeer asked warily.

"The truth." Penrose's sincerity was evident. "A young woman who recognized fraud and corruption, who documented crimes at great personal risk, and who died pursuing justice for vulnerable immigrants. Her story should inspire reform, not just provide entertainment for gossip columns."

"And the trial?" Theodore pressed. "Your coverage could influence public opinion."

"Which is precisely why I want to get the facts right." Penrose pulled out a photograph, Charlotte at some society event, smiling at the camera with intelligence and humor evident in her eyes. "This is who she was. Not a hysterical girl who killed herself over a broken engagement, but a woman who chose truth over safety."

Lillian felt unexpected emotion as she looked at the photograph. She'd never met Charlotte alive, had only encountered her death, her journal, and the aftermath of her courage. Seeing her vibrant and living, even in a frozen moment captured by a camera, made the loss feel more profound.

"Tell her story," Katherine said quietly. "Tell them all about Charlotte. About what she discovered, what she risked, why she died. Make sure her death means something beyond convicting Harrison."

"I will." Penrose made a note in his book. "And the immigrant families? The ones who were defrauded?"

"Special Agent Loomis is working to identify all the victims," Blackwood reported. "The Treasury Department plans to recover as much of the stolen money as possible from Harrison and his associates' assets."

"That will take years," Mrs. Duval observed pragmatically. "Legal proceedings, asset seizures, claims processing, these families won't see restitution for a long time, if ever."

"Which is why I'm establishing a fund," Theodore said. The announcement surprised everyone in the room. "The Charlotte Vandermeer Memorial Fund, dedicated to assisting immigrant families who've been victimized by fraud. It won't undo what Harrison did, but perhaps it can help prevent future victims."

Mrs. Vandermeer's eyes filled with tears, but she smiled through them. "Charlotte would have approved. She always believed wealth carried responsibility, not just privilege."

As Penrose took notes and asked careful questions about Charlotte's investigation, Lillian found herself reflecting on how cases transformed everyone they touched. The Vandermeers had lost a daughter but gained purpose. Katherine had survived trauma but emerged stronger and more committed to justice. Even Theodore's public testimony about his own investment with Harrison would help others recognize warning signs of fraud.

"Miss Cross?" Katherine drew her aside as the others continued their discussion with Penrose. "I wanted to thank you properly. For everything you risked to find the truth about Charlotte's death."

"You don't need to thank me. Justice for your sister—"

"Isn't just about Charlotte anymore," Katherine interrupted gently. "It's about every family Harrison defrauded, every woman who's been told her questions don't matter, every person who believed the powerful were untouchable. You proved they're not."

"We proved it together," Lillian corrected. "Your courage in that basement, your testimony—"

"Wouldn't have mattered if you hadn't built the case that forced them into that confrontation." Katherine smiled, and for a moment Lillian could see Charlotte in her features, the same determination, the same refusal to accept easy lies. "Charlotte wrote in her journal that she hoped someone would continue asking questions after she was gone. You did. You gave her death meaning."

As the afternoon wore on and the discussion shifted to trial preparation and memorial plans, Lillian felt the satisfaction that came at the end of successful investigations. Not the triumphant joy of adventure novels, but the quieter knowledge that truth had been pursued and partially achieved.

Detective Blackwood found her standing by the window, looking out at Fifth Avenue where expensive carriages passed in endless procession.

"Thinking about the next case?" he asked.

"Thinking about this one." Lillian turned to face him, noting how the afternoon light softened his usually serious features. "Charlotte died because she asked questions that powerful men didn't want answered. How many other women have died for the same reason? How many injustices remain hidden because investigating them seems too dangerous?"

"Probably thousands." Blackwood's honesty was one of the things she valued most about him. "But we can't solve every injustice, Lillian. We can only address the ones in front of us."

"Is that enough?"

"It has to be. Otherwise, the scope of the problem becomes paralyzing." He moved to stand beside her at the window. "Charlotte's death mattered because we made it matter. Katherine's survival mattered because we refused to accept that powerful men were untouchable. That's enough for today."

"And tomorrow?"

"Tomorrow, there will be other cases. Other victims who need someone to ask uncomfortable questions." His smile carried warmth. "Fortunately, asking uncomfortable questions seems to be your particular talent."

Before Lillian could respond, Mrs. Duval approached with her characteristic perfect timing.

"I hate to interrupt what appears to be a moment, but I've just received word that the federal grand jury has formally indicted Harrison and his associates. The trial is scheduled for next month."

"Next month?" Lillian was surprised by the speed.

"Agent Loomis insisted on expedited proceedings. Something about not giving wealthy defendants time to manipulate evidence or intimidate witnesses." Mrs. Duval's smile was satisfied. "He's also requested that you serve as an expert witness regarding the forensic evidence of Charlotte's murder."

"Me? I'm not officially qualified—"

"You examined both bodies involved in this case, documented evidence that official authorities overlooked, and built the forensic timeline that proves premeditation." Mrs. Duval's tone brooked no argument. "You're perfectly qualified, and Morrison knows it. So does the district attorney."

As they prepared to leave the Vandermeer mansion, Katherine intercepted them at the door.

"Miss Cross, one more thing. Charlotte's journal, the one she kept documenting Harrison's crimes. What will happen to it?"

"It's evidence," Blackwood explained. "It'll be retained by the court until after the trial."

"And then?"

"Then it should be returned to your family."

Katherine shook her head. "I want you to keep it. Or perhaps donate it to one of the reform organizations working to protect immigrant families. Charlotte wrote it as a warning and a call to action. It shouldn't be locked away in our family archives where only Vandermeers will read it."

"Are you certain?" Lillian asked. "It's the last direct connection to your sister's thoughts and feelings."

"Which is exactly why it needs to be shared." Katherine's determination was absolute. "Charlotte died trying to expose corruption. The least we can do is ensure her work continues long after the trial ends."

As they emerged onto Fifth Avenue, where their more modest carriage waited among the gleaming coaches of Manhattan's elite, Lillian reflected on how far they'd come since the charity gala where Katherine had first approached them. Then, they'd been investigating a suspicious suicide. Now, they'd exposed a massive fraud conspiracy, brought three murderers to justice, and potentially inspired reforms that could protect countless vulnerable families.

"You're quiet," Blackwood observed as they settled into the carriage.

"I'm thinking about Charlotte's journal. About how her words will outlive her, will continue inspiring reform and justice long after we're all gone."

"A legacy worth dying for?" Mrs. Duval asked gently.

"A legacy worth living for," Lillian corrected. "Charlotte died for the truth. We have the luxury of continuing her work while still breathing."

As the carriage rattled toward their office, where no doubt other cases and other victims awaited their attention, Lillian felt the weight and privilege of her chosen profession. She'd started as a mortician's daughter who examined the dead to understand how they'd died. Now she was an investigator who fought for the living, ensuring that death—when it came through violence and injustice—would be answered with truth and consequences.

Charlotte Vandermeer's gilded corpse had revealed more than just a murder. It had exposed a society where wealth corrupted, where power protected criminals, and where asking questions could be fatal. But it had also proven that truth, persistently pursued, could topple even the most carefully constructed lies.

The case was closed. Justice, imperfect but real, had been served.

And somewhere, Lillian hoped, Charlotte

Vandermeer rested easier knowing her death had not been in vain.

ASHES
IN THE
TENEMENT

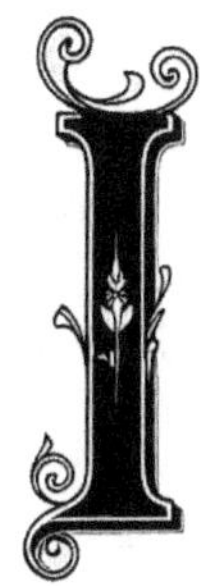

The telegram arrived at Cross & Associates just after dawn, delivered by a breathless messenger boy whose ash-stained clothes and soot-streaked face told part of the story before Lillian Cross even broke the seal. Her hands trembled slightly as she unfolded the paper—not from the November cold seeping through the office windows, but from a premonition that whatever news the telegram carried would change everything.

Fire at Mulberry Street tenement. Catastrophic loss of life. Police declaring accident. Bodies showing signs inconsistent with official narrative. Come immediately. Your expertise urgently needed. - E.C.

Lillian read it twice, her father's careful handwriting, transcribed by some harried telegram clerk, burning itself into her memory. Edmund Cross was not a man prone to dramatics. In thirty years running Cross

& Sons Funeral Parlor, he'd developed an almost preternatural calm in the face of death. If he was summoning her with words like "catastrophic" and "urgently needed," something was profoundly wrong.

"Bad news?" Detective Nathaniel Blackwood looked up from the financial ledgers he'd been reviewing, evidence for the upcoming Harrison Ashford trial that would begin in just three days. The trial that had already consumed weeks of their lives and promised to expose one of Manhattan's most elaborate fraud conspiracies.

"The worst kind." Lillian grabbed her coat and medical bag, her investigative instincts overriding the exhaustion that had settled into her bones after six weeks of intensive case preparation. "There's been a fire in the Lower East Side. My father says the bodies are telling a story the police don't want to hear."

Blackwood was already on his feet, his Irish accent thickening slightly with concern as it always did when danger threatened. "How many dead?"

"He doesn't say exactly. Just 'catastrophic loss of life.'" The phrase felt obscene in its clinical distance. Lillian forced herself to think like an investigator rather than someone about to confront tragedy on a scale she'd never witnessed. "Mulberry Street—that's the Italian district. The tenements there pack families into spaces barely fit for rats."

"Wooden buildings constructed as cheaply as possible and maintained even less," Blackwood added grimly, shrugging into his own coat. "A fire in those conditions wouldn't just kill, it would massacre."

Mrs. Margaret Duval arrived as they were preparing to leave, her elegant carriage stopping outside their modest office with the precision of someone whose schedule never varied. But one look at their faces and she understood immediately that normal plans had been shattered.

"What's happened?"

"Tenement fire. Multiple deaths. Suspicious circumstances." Lillian showed her the telegram. "My father never uses words like 'catastrophic' unless he means them literally."

Mrs. Duval's expression shifted from social pleasantness to the sharp focus she brought to their investigations. Since helping expose Mrs. Whitmore's criminal network and then Charlotte Vandermeer's murder, she'd become an essential part of their team, providing social connections, financial resources, and a practical ruthlessness that balanced Lillian's forensic precision and Blackwood's detective work.

"I'm coming with you," she said, not a question. "If this is connected to anything we've been investigating…"

"Why would a tenement fire be connected to Harrison's fraud trial?" Blackwood asked.

"Because Harrison didn't work alone," Mrs. Duval replied. "We exposed him and Robert Thornton, but there are other wealthy men involved in that conspiracy. Men with investments in real estate, shipping, construction, all the businesses that exploit immigrant communities."

The implication hung in the air between them. They'd dismantled part of a criminal network, but networks had a way of fighting back. And if someone wanted to eliminate witnesses who might testify about fraud, embezzlement, and corruption…

"We're speculating," Lillian said firmly, though the same thoughts had occurred to her. "Let's see what Father has found before we start connecting cases that might not be connected."

The cab ride to Mulberry Street felt both too long and too short. Lillian used the time to mentally prepare herself, reviewing what she knew about fire deaths, burn patterns, smoke inhalation. But no amount of academic knowledge could truly prepare someone for witnessing mass tragedy.

The November morning was bitter cold, the kind of day where breath crystallized in the air and fingers went numb within minutes. But as they traveled south toward the Lower East Side, cold became the least of their concerns. Even blocks away, they could see it—a column of smoke still rising above the tenement rooftops, darker and thicker than the normal haze of coal fires and factory smokestacks.

"Dear God," Mrs. Duval breathed. "The whole building must have—"

She didn't finish. Couldn't finish. Because as their cab turned onto Mulberry Street, the scope of the disaster became horrifyingly clear.

The tenement, five stories of timber and hope that had housed perhaps fifty families, was now a blackened skeleton. Charred timbers jutted toward the gray November sky like the ribs of some immense beast picked clean by scavengers. What had been home to hundreds of immigrants was now little more than a monument to how quickly life could be consumed by flames.

But it was the people that made Lillian's breath catch in her throat.

Survivors huddled in clusters along the street, wrapped in blankets provided by charity workers whose presence suggested they'd been here for hours. Women wailed in Italian, their grief needing no translation. Children sat silent and staring, too young to process what they'd lost but old enough to understand it was everything. Men stood apart, their faces blank with the particular numbness that came from witnessing horror beyond comprehension.

And the bodies. Even from the cab, Lillian could see them, covered forms laid out in rows near what had once been the building's entrance. Not the organized efficiency of a funeral parlor, but the desperate triage of a disaster scene where the living took priority and the dead waited their turn for attention.

"How many?" Blackwood asked quietly, though he was already counting.

"Twenty visible from here," Lillian replied. "But if the building was fully occupied when the fire started…"

She didn't need to finish. They all understood the mathematics of tragedy, five floors, ten rooms per floor, six to eight people per room. A fire that started after midnight when families were asleep would have killed dozens before most even woke to realize they were in danger.

Their cab couldn't navigate any closer, the street was choked with fire equipment, police wagons, and the crowds of survivors, rescuers, and gawkers that disaster always attracted. They climbed out and began working their way toward the center of the scene, where Lillian could see her father's familiar figure speaking with a fire official.

Edmund Cross looked older than she'd ever seen him. Soot streaked his face, his clothes were smoke-stained, and his hands trembled slightly as he gestured toward the ruins. But what struck Lillian most was his expression, not the professional neutrality he maintained around death, but barely controlled fury.

"Father." She approached quickly, noting how relief flooded his features when he saw her.

"Thank God. I wasn't certain the telegram would reach you in time." Edmund pulled her slightly away from the fire official, lowering his voice. "Lillian, something is wrong here. Profoundly wrong."

"Tell me."

Edmund glanced around to ensure they wouldn't be overheard, then pulled out a handkerchief and wiped ash from his face, a gesture that seemed more about buying time to organize his thoughts than actual cleaning. "I've been here since just before dawn. The fire started around three o'clock this morning. By the time the fire companies arrived, the entire building was engulfed."

"Where were you when it started?" Blackwood asked.

"At home. But Mrs. Lucia Moretti, she does laundry for several families near here—she came to the funeral parlor around four o'clock, hysterical. Her daughter lived in this building with her husband and children. She was begging me to help identify bodies when they were recovered." Edmund's voice tightened. "I've been examining the dead as they're brought out. Twenty-three so far, with at least fifteen more still inside."

"Thirty-eight dead?" Mrs. Duval's horror was evident. "In a single building?"

"Perhaps more. The survivors are still being accounted for, but many families are entirely unaccounted for." Edmund's hands clenched into fists. "But Lillian, that's not what I need you to see. It's how they died."

He led them toward a makeshift examination area that had been set up in a warehouse across the street. Inside, away from the crowds and chaos, several bodies had been arranged for official identification and documentation. The city's medical examiner hadn't yet arrived—or perhaps hadn't been called, given the authorities' apparent eagerness to declare this a simple accident.

Lillian approached the first body with the clinical detachment she'd learned in her father's preparation room. But clinical detachment could only do so much when faced with a child no more than five years old, her small body showing the unmistakable signs of fire death.

"The burn patterns," Edmund said quietly, pointing. "Look at her back versus her front."

Lillian studied the body carefully, her forensic training asserting itself over emotion. The child's front showed moderate burning consistent with radiant heat exposure. But her back…

"The burns are much deeper on her posterior surface," Lillian observed, pulling out her magnifying glass. "As if she was lying down when the fire reached her."

"Exactly. Now look at this." Edmund moved to an adult male, perhaps thirty years old. "He was found near the third-floor stairwell. Official theory is he was trying to escape when he collapsed from smoke inhalation."

But the body told a different story. Lillian examined the man's hands, his face, the positioning of his limbs. "No defensive wounds. No soot in what remains of his nasal passages—at least not in the density you'd expect from someone conscious and breathing in a smoke-filled building."

"I found the same pattern in four other bodies," Edmund said. "Burns suggesting they were already prone or unconscious when the fire reached them. Lack of the typical defensive postures or respiratory evidence you'd expect from people dying in their sleep from smoke inhalation."

Blackwood had been examining other bodies, his detective's instincts engaged despite the grimness of the task. "Could they have been overcome by smoke before the fire reached them?"

"That's what the police are suggesting," Edmund replied. "But smoke inhalation deaths show specific patterns—soot in the airways, carbon monoxide in the blood that creates a characteristic coloring. Several of these bodies don't show those signs."

"Then what killed them?" Mrs. Duval asked.

"I don't know yet. I'd need to conduct proper examinations, not just these preliminary assessments." Edmund's frustration was evident. "But the authorities have already decided this was an accident, overcrowded tenement, knocked-over lamp, tragic but simple explanation."

"Except the evidence suggests otherwise," Lillian said slowly, her mind working through possibilities. "Father, if people were already dead or unconscious before the fire reached them…"

"Then someone killed them first, then set the fire to cover the murders."

The words hung in the cold warehouse air like a physical presence. Mass murder disguised as accident. Dozens of people killed and then burned to hide the evidence.

A commotion outside drew their attention, raised voices, the sound of official authority being asserted. Lillian moved to the warehouse door and saw a well-dressed man arguing with the fire marshal, his gestures expansive and his tone carrying the confidence of someone accustomed to being obeyed.

"Who's that?" she asked.

Edmund's expression darkened. "William Hartley. He owns this building, along with half the tenements on this block."

Lillian's blood turned to ice. William Hartley, one of Harrison Ashford's associates in the fraud conspiracy. The same William Hartley who stood to lose everything if witnesses testified at the trial beginning in three days. The same William Hartley whose real estate empire was built on overcrowded tenements and minimal maintenance.

"This isn't coincidence," Blackwood said quietly. "The timing, Hartley's presence, the suspicious death patterns…"

"We need to examine the fire scene," Lillian said, already formulating an investigation plan. "If this was arson, there will be evidence. Accelerant patterns, point of origin inconsistent with an accidental lamp fire, structural damage that tells a story."

"The building is officially too dangerous to enter," Edmund warned. "Fire marshal has declared it an imminent collapse risk."

"Then we'll need to be unofficial," Lillian replied, watching as Hartley continued his animated conversation with fire officials. "And quick. Before evidence is destroyed or the building is demolished."

As they prepared to leave the warehouse, a young woman approached them, her clothing ash-stained, her face streaked with tears and soot, but her eyes burning with a fury that transcended grief.

"You're the investigators," she said in accented English. "The ones who caught that rich woman who killed people. Mrs. Moretti told me you would come."

"I'm Lillian Cross. This is Detective Blackwood and Mrs. Duval. And you are?"

"Rosa Ferrante." The woman's voice was steady despite the tears tracking through the ash on her face. "I lived on the third floor with my husband Carlo and our three children. Last night, I was visiting my sister in Brooklyn with my two older children. But Carlo and our youngest son Antonio—they were home when the fire started."

Her voice finally broke on her son's name. Lillian felt her chest constrict with sympathy and rage in equal measure.

"I'm so sorry for your loss, Mrs. Ferrante."

"Save your sorrow," Rosa said with unexpected steel. "I want justice. The police are calling this an accident, but it wasn't. It couldn't have been."

"What makes you say that?" Blackwood asked gently.

Rosa looked toward the burned building, then back at them with absolute certainty. "Because last night, before I left for my sister's house, I saw two men coming out of the basement. Well-dressed men who didn't live in our building. They were moving fast, like they were running from something. And twenty minutes later, I smelled something chemical. Not lamp oil, something sharper, more bitter."

Lillian felt the pieces beginning to fall into place. "Did you tell the police?"

"I tried. They said I was confused, traumatized, that I probably saw residents trying to escape and my memory was playing tricks." Rosa's hands clenched into fists. "But I know what I saw. Those men set the fire. And Mr. Hartley…" she pointed toward where the real estate magnate stood, "…is here to make sure nobody believes people like me."

As if sensing he was being discussed, Hartley's attention shifted toward their group. His expression darkened when he recognized Lillian and Blackwood, they'd testified in preliminary hearings for the Ashford trial, their faces now known to everyone involved in that conspiracy.

For a long moment, their eyes locked across the disaster scene. Hartley's face carried the cold calculation of a man assessing a threat. Then he smiled—a gesture that held no warmth, only acknowledgment that they were now adversaries in a game whose stakes included dozens of lives.

"He knows we're investigating," Mrs. Duval observed quietly.

"Good," Lillian replied, her determination crystallizing into purpose. "Let him know. Let him understand that we won't be intimidated and we won't stop until we prove what really happened here."

As the November morning wore on and the death toll continued to rise, Lillian understood with absolute clarity that this investigation would be different from anything they'd faced before. Charlotte Vandermeer's murder had been personal tragedy amplified by elite conspiracy. But Mulberry Street was massacre, mass murder disguised as accident, and it was just the beginning of understanding how far wealthy criminals would go to protect their secrets.

The ashes held their stories. All she had to do was learn how to read them before they were swept away forever.

The fire marshal's office was a cramped space in a building that smelled of smoke, sweat, and bureaucratic indifference. Marshal Patrick O'Brien sat behind a desk piled with reports, maps, and what appeared to be the remains of someone's lunch, looking every bit as exhausted as Lillian felt.

"Absolutely not," he said before Detective Blackwood had even finished his request. "The structure is unstable. Could collapse at any moment. I'm not authorizing anyone to enter for any reason."

"We only need access to the basement," Lillian pressed. "Just enough time to document evidence before—"

"Before what? Before the building kills you like

it killed those poor souls last night?" O'Brien's frustration was genuine, not the calculated obstruction of someone being paid to look the other way. "I've got thirty-seven bodies, dozens of families homeless, and a building that's one strong wind away from burying half of Mulberry Street in rubble. Your investigation will have to wait for safety."

"By which time any evidence of arson will be destroyed," Blackwood said.

O'Brien's expression flickered with something, uncertainty, perhaps, or recognition. "You think it was set deliberately?"

"We have an eyewitness who saw two men leaving the basement shortly before the fire started," Lillian said, pulling out her notes. "And forensic evidence suggesting accelerant was used. But if you demolish the building before we can properly examine…"

"Then thirty-seven murders get written off as an accident," Blackwood finished.

The marshal rubbed his face wearily. "Even if I believed you, and I'm not saying I don't, I can't authorize entry. The building inspector declared it an imminent collapse hazard. If I let you in and you get killed, that's on my conscience. And my career."

"What if we went in without authorization?" Lillian asked. "Hypothetically."

O'Brien's eyes narrowed. "Hypothetically, I'd have to report you for trespassing and endangering public safety. But…" he paused, choosing his words carefully, "…I also can't watch that building twenty-four hours a day. Especially not tonight, when I'll be at my daughter's birthday party from six o'clock until at least nine."

The message was clear. Blackwood nodded slowly. "What time does the demolition crew arrive tomorrow?"

"First light. Seven o'clock sharp." O'Brien stood,

signaling the conversation was over. "I'd hate for anyone to be foolish enough to enter that building after dark when no one's watching. Extremely dangerous. Could get themselves killed and create all sorts of paperwork for me."

As they left the marshal's office, Lillian felt equal parts gratitude and apprehension. O'Brien was giving them a window, one night to find evidence that could prove arson or lose it forever to demolition.

"We'll need equipment," Blackwood said as they emerged onto the street. "Lamps, tools to dig through debris, something to document what we find."

"And someone who knows the building's layout," Lillian added. "Even if the structure's been damaged, we'll need to know where we're going."

"Mrs. Ferrante lived there for three years," Edmund said. He'd been waiting outside the marshal's office, maintaining the fiction that he wasn't involved in planning anything that might be considered trespassing. "She knows every floor, every room."

"We can't ask her to go back into the building where her husband and son died," Lillian protested.

"You won't have to ask." Rosa Ferrante stepped from the doorway of a nearby shop where she'd apparently been waiting. "I heard what the marshal said. I'm coming with you tonight."

"Mrs. Ferrante…"

"Don't." Rosa's voice was firm. "Those men killed my family. If there's evidence in that basement that can prove it, I'm going to help you find it. Carlo would expect nothing less."

Lillian recognized the expression on Rosa's face, the same determination she'd seen in Katherine Vandermeer's eyes when the younger woman had insisted on helping investigate her sister's murder. Grief transformed into purpose, loss channeled into action.

"Then we meet at ten o'clock tonight,"

Blackwood said. "Away from the building, we don't want to draw attention by gathering near the ruins."

"There's an alley two blocks south," Rosa said. "Behind the butcher shop. Nobody goes there after dark."

They separated to make preparations, agreeing to reconvene at the designated location. Lillian returned to Cross & Associates to gather supplies, her mind already cataloging what they'd need for their unauthorized investigation.

Mrs. Duval was waiting in the office, having heard about the fire through her extensive network of society connections.

"Thirty-seven dead," she said without preamble. "And William Hartley's name is all over it. This isn't coincidence, Lillian."

"I know." Lillian began pulling equipment from cabinets, her medical bag, examination tools, sample containers, a portable lantern. "Hartley and Harrison were partners in fraud. Now we're supposed to believe it's coincidence that Hartley's building burns the same week Harrison's trial begins?"

"You think the fire is connected to the trial?"

"I think Hartley is destroying evidence. His buildings, his business records, any documentation that might connect him to Harrison's fraud network." Lillian paused, considering. "And killing witnesses who might testify."

Mrs. Duval's face went pale. "The fire killed potential witnesses?"

"We won't know until we examine who died and whether any of them had knowledge of Hartley's business dealings. But the timing is suspicious."

"When do you examine the building?"

"Tonight. After dark. Without official permission." Lillian met Mrs. Duval's eyes. "Which means if we're caught, we'll face criminal charges."

"Then don't get caught." Mrs. Duval's pragmatism was reassuring. "What can I do to help?"

"Keep your distance. If this goes wrong, we'll need someone with social standing and resources to advocate for our release." Lillian pulled on her warmest coat, knowing the night would be cold. "And if we find evidence of arson, we'll need it documented and delivered to someone who can't be intimidated by Hartley's attorneys."

"Special Agent Loomis," Mrs. Duval suggested. "He handled the federal investigation into Harrison's fraud. He'd be the right person to receive evidence of murder connected to that case."

They finalized their plans, and Lillian spent the afternoon reviewing everything she knew about fire investigation and arson detection. Edmund provided notes from his examination of the bodies, documenting the inconsistencies he'd observed. Each piece of evidence pointed toward the same conclusion: the Mulberry Street fire had been deliberately set, and William Hartley was involved.

As twilight fell over Manhattan, Lillian made her way to the designated meeting point. The alley behind the butcher shop was dark and damp, smelling of blood and refuse, but it provided cover from the street. Blackwood arrived first, carrying a canvas bag filled with tools and equipment. Rosa appeared moments later, dressed in dark clothing and moving with the cautious determination of someone confronting their worst nightmares.

"The fire started in the basement," Rosa said without preamble. "That's where those men were. If we're going to find evidence, that's where we need to look."

"Lead the way," Blackwood said.

The walk to the burned tenement felt surreal, moving through streets Lillian had known her entire life, but transformed by darkness and purpose into something foreign and dangerous. The building itself loomed against the night sky like a monument to tragedy, its blackened shell a reminder of how quickly life could be consumed.

The fire crews had departed hours ago, leaving only a single police officer standing watch at the front entrance. But Rosa led them around the block to a narrow gap between buildings, the kind of space that tenement residents used for everything from storage to illegal activities.

"There's a service entrance in the back," Rosa whispered. "The police won't be watching it."

They squeezed through the gap, their clothes catching on rough brick and splintered wood. The rear of the building was even more damaged than the front, the fire having started low and burned upward with devastating efficiency.

The service entrance was little more than a hole in the wall where a door had once hung. Blackwood lit their lantern carefully, keeping the light low and shielded. Inside, the destruction was total, charred timbers, collapsed floors, and the pervasive smell of burned wood and worse.

"The basement stairs are this way," Rosa said, her voice steady despite obvious fear. "Or they were. I don't know what the fire left."

They picked their way through debris, testing each step before committing weight to it. The building groaned around them like a dying thing, and Lillian was acutely aware of how the marshal's warnings about structural instability weren't exaggeration, they were understatement.

The basement stairs had partially collapsed, but enough remained to allow careful descent. Blackwood went first, testing each step and warning them about weak points. Rosa followed, moving with the automatic knowledge of someone who'd used these stairs hundreds of times. Lillian came last, her medical bag bouncing against her hip and her heart pounding with equal parts excitement and terror.

The basement was a cavern of shadows and destruction. Water from the fire crews' hoses had pooled in low spots, mixing with ash to create a black sludge that sucked at their boots. But despite the damage, some structures remained—support columns, portions of walls, and most importantly, the areas where the fire had burned hottest.

"There." Rosa pointed to a corner where the stone foundation showed distinct scorch patterns. "That's where I saw the men. Near the coal storage area."

They approached carefully, Blackwood holding the lantern high while Lillian examined the area with her magnifying glass. The burn patterns were immediately suspicious, too uniform, too intense for a fire that had supposedly started from an overturned lamp upstairs.

"This is the point of origin," she said, taking samples of the ash and debris. "The fire started here and spread upward."

"Which contradicts the official story," Blackwood observed. "They're saying it started on the third floor."

"Because that's where they found the overturned lamp that supposedly caused it." Rosa's voice carried bitter understanding. "But the lamp was planted. I never kept lamps in the bedroom, Carlo forbade it after hearing about tenement fires."

Lillian found what she'd been hoping for, a section of floor that showed clear evidence of accelerant. The burn pattern was too deep, too concentrated, speaking of something more volatile than lamp oil.

"Look at this." She scraped samples into glass

vials, labeling each carefully. "This is paraffin or kerosene, applied deliberately in patterns designed to spread fire quickly."

A sound from above, footsteps, multiple sets, moving through the ruins with purpose, made them all freeze.

"The police?" Rosa whispered.

"Or Hartley's people." Blackwood extinguished the lantern immediately, plunging them into darkness. "Either way, we need to leave. Now."

But the footsteps were between them and their exit route, moving with the systematic efficiency of a search pattern. They'd been discovered.

"This way." Rosa's hand found Lillian's in the darkness. "There's another way out. Through the coal chute."

They felt their way through the basement, guided by Rosa's intimate knowledge of the building's layout. Behind them, Lillian could hear voices, low, urgent, coordinating their search.

"Someone's down here. Spread out and find them."

The coal chute was a narrow opening that led to a chute running up to street level—designed for deliveries but rarely used in recent years. Rosa showed them how to brace themselves against the walls and climb, using the rough stone for purchase.

It was slow, claustrophobic work, made worse by the darkness and the knowledge that their pursuers were getting closer. Lillian's medical bag kept catching on rough edges, and several times she thought she'd have to abandon it. But finally, blessedly, she saw starlight above, the chute's street-level opening.

They emerged in an alley three buildings away from the fire scene, covered in soot and ash, their hands scraped raw from climbing. Behind them, they could hear more sounds of search in the basement, but the sounds were fading as their pursuers realized they'd escaped.

"Did you get what you needed?" Rosa asked, breathing hard from exertion and fear.

Lillian checked her medical bag. The sample vials were intact, her notes preserved. "Yes. Enough to prove the fire was deliberately set."

"Then it was worth it." Rosa's smile was grim. "Now what?"

"Now we take this evidence to someone who can't be intimidated or bought off," Blackwood said.

"And we prove that William Hartley murdered thirty-seven people to protect his criminal empire."

As they made their way through the dark streets toward safety, Lillian felt the familiar weight of an investigation reaching its critical phase. They had evidence, they had witnesses, and they had proof that connected Hartley to mass murder.

But Hartley had proven he was willing to kill to protect his secrets. And now he knew they were investigating, knew they'd found evidence he'd tried to destroy.

The real danger was just beginning.

The basement of Cross & Sons Funeral Parlor had never felt more like a sanctuary than it did at three o'clock in the morning. Lillian spread her collected evidence across the marble preparation table, careful not to contaminate the samples she'd risked her life to obtain. The gas lamps cast steady light across charred fragments, ash-stained vials, and her hastily scrawled notes from the tenement basement.

Detective Blackwood paced the length of the preparation room, still too agitated from their narrow escape to sit still. Rosa Ferrante had collapsed into a chair near the wall, exhaustion and grief finally overwhelming the determination that had sustained her through the night's dangers.

"The accelerant is definitely paraffin-based," Lillian said, examining a sample under her father's microscope. "See these crystalline structures? They're consistent with commercial lamp fuel, but applied in quantities and patterns that could only be deliberate."

"Commercial lamp fuel," Blackwood repeated. "The kind anyone could purchase at any general store in the city."

"Which makes it nearly impossible to trace to a specific buyer." Lillian's frustration was evident. "Hartley's people were careful about that, at least."

Edmund descended the stairs carrying a tea tray, his solution to most crises, and set it on a side table. "You'll need to connect the evidence to Hartley directly. Proving the fire was arson isn't enough if you can't demonstrate who set it."

"Rosa saw two well-dressed men leaving the basement," Blackwood argued. "That's witness testimony."

"Which Hartley's attorneys will dismiss as the confused recollections of a traumatized immigrant woman." Edmund's pragmatism was harsh but accurate. "You need more than physical evidence and eyewitness accounts. You need motive and means that point specifically to Hartley."

Lillian knew her father was right. The Charlotte Vandermeer case had taught her that wealthy men insulated themselves with layers of deniability. Harrison hadn't personally murdered Charlotte, he'd arranged it through others. Hartley would have done the same.

"We need to understand who died in that fire," she said slowly, an idea forming. "Not just how many, but who specifically. If Hartley was eliminating witnesses who could testify about his criminal activities…"

"Then the victims' identities would reveal the motive." Blackwood stopped pacing, his detective instincts engaged. "The fire marshal's office will have a list of the deceased."

"Official records that Hartley has probably already influenced," Rosa said bitterly. She'd been so quiet that they'd almost forgotten she was there. "But the community knows. We know who lived in each room, who was home that night, who escaped and who didn't."

"Can you compile a list?" Lillian asked gently.

Rosa nodded, though her expression was haunted. "The Ferrettis on the first floor, both parents and their baby. The Greco family on the second, five children, only two survived. The Marinos, the Russos, the Lombardis…" Her voice broke. "I can name them all. Every family, every person who burned because Hartley packed us into a deathtrap and then set it on fire."

As Rosa recited names from memory, Lillian wrote them down, creating a list that transformed statistics into people. Thirty-seven dead became parents and children, workers and grandmothers, each with their own stories that had ended in flames.

"Wait," Blackwood said, studying the list. "Go back. You said the Marino family, what did the father do for work?"

"Vincenzo Marino? He worked on the docks. Loading and unloading cargo from ships." Rosa's brow furrowed. "Why?"

"Because dock work puts him in contact with shipping manifests, customs records, cargo inventories." Blackwood pulled out his notebook from the Harrison Ashford investigation. "Hartley's real estate empire is built on money from somewhere. During the Vandermeer investigation, we discovered Harrison was laundering money through various businesses, but we never fully traced where the original money came from."

"You think it came from smuggling?" Lillian asked, following his logic.

"Shipping companies bring in more than legitimate cargo. If someone knows what to look for, they could document illegal imports, stolen goods, contraband, items brought in without paying customs duties." Blackwood's excitement was building. "A dock worker who handled cargo for Hartley's shipping partners might have seen something incriminating."

"And if that dock worker lived in a building Hartley owned and started asking uncomfortable questions…" Edmund's expression was grim.

"He'd become a liability that needed to be eliminated." Lillian returned to her list, looking at it with new understanding. "Who else on this list might have had knowledge of Hartley's business dealings?"

Rosa studied the names, her face growing pale as connections became clear. "Maria Russo worked as a seamstress. She did alterations for wealthy families, including… oh God, including the Hartley household. She came home two weeks ago saying she'd overheard Mr. Hartley arguing with business associates about money and something going missing from inventory."

"What else did she overhear?"

"I don't know. She was frightened, said she'd heard too much and was worried about keeping her position." Rosa's hands trembled as she reached for the tea Edmund had prepared. "I told her not to worry, that wealthy people always argued about money. I never thought…"

"You couldn't have known," Lillian said gently. "What about others on the list?"

As they worked through the names, a pattern emerged. Not everyone who died had direct knowledge of Hartley's criminal activities, many were simply residents who'd been home when the fire started. But several names stood out: the dock worker who handled shipping manifests, the seamstress who'd overheard incriminating conversations, a bookkeeper who'd briefly worked for one of Hartley's business fronts before being dismissed for asking questions about irregular accounts.

"He didn't just set fire to a building," Blackwood said with cold fury. "He orchestrated a mass killing disguised as an accident, eliminating multiple witnesses while making it look like typical tenement tragedy."

"And the timing," Lillian added, consulting the calendar on her father's desk. "Harrison's trial starts in three days. These witnesses couldn't testify about Harrison directly, but they could have provided evidence about Hartley's role in the larger conspiracy."

"Which means the federal prosecutors don't know about these potential witnesses," Edmund observed. "If they did, they'd have protection in place."

"Or Hartley would have waited until after the trial to eliminate them." Blackwood's expression was dark. "He acted now because he knew the prosecution was close to discovering the connection."

A knock at the preparation room door made them all freeze. Edmund moved to answer it, while Lillian quickly covered their evidence with a cloth, midnight investigations and forensic analysis weren't illegal, exactly, but explaining them at three in the morning would raise uncomfortable questions.

Mrs. Margaret Duval swept into the room with the energy of someone who'd never heard of proper sleeping hours. "I've just come from Agent Loomis's home. I hope you'll forgive the intrusion at this ungodly hour, but I thought you'd want to know—the federal investigators have moved up their timeline for the Ashford trial. They're calling their first witnesses tomorrow morning instead of next week."

"Why the sudden change?" Blackwood asked.

"Because someone has been threatening

potential witnesses." Mrs. Duval's expression was grim. "Two immigrant families who were prepared to testify about Harrison's fraud schemes have suddenly refused to cooperate. Both cited fear for their safety, and both lived in buildings owned by William Hartley."

"Not the Mulberry Street building?" Lillian asked urgently.

"No, but similar tenements in the same district." Mrs. Duval looked at their evidence-covered table with understanding. "The fire wasn't just about eliminating witnesses, it was about terrifying the survivors. Showing anyone who might consider testifying what happens to people who cooperate with authorities."

The pieces were falling into place with horrifying clarity. Hartley hadn't just committed mass murder to hide evidence, he'd done it to intimidate an entire community into silence.

"We need to get this evidence to Agent Loomis immediately," Lillian said, gathering her samples and notes. "Along with the list of victims and their connections to Hartley's criminal activities."

"It's three-thirty in the morning," Edmund protested.

"And the demolition crew arrives at seven," Blackwood countered. "Once that building is knocked down, any evidence we missed is gone forever. We need federal investigators securing that site now, tonight, before Hartley can destroy anything else."

Mrs. Duval was already moving toward the door. "My carriage is waiting. Agent Loomis lives in Brooklyn, we can be there within the hour if we hurry."

As they prepared to leave, Rosa stood with obvious determination. "I'm coming with you."

"Mrs. Ferrante, you've already risked so much."

"Those men killed my husband and son, and they terrified an entire community into silence." Rosa's voice was steady despite her tears. "I won't hide while you fight for justice. If Agent Loomis needs witness testimony, I'll provide it. If the prosecutors need someone who can identify victims and explain their connection to Hartley, I'll do that too."

Lillian recognized the transformation she'd seen before in Katherine Vandermeer and countless other women who'd suffered injustice, grief crystallizing into purpose, fear transmuting into courage.

"Then let's go," she said.

The journey to Brooklyn was cold and dark, their carriage rattling through streets that were empty except for night workers and the occasional police officer on patrol. Lillian used the time to organize her evidence and notes, preparing to present a coherent case to Agent Loomis.

"Do you think he'll believe us?" Rosa asked quietly. "A mortician's daughter, an Irish detective, and an Italian immigrant woman, we're not exactly the kind of witnesses federal agents usually trust."

"Agent Loomis's mother was Irish," Blackwood replied. "He understands what it means to be dismissed because of where you came from. That's why he became a federal agent, to protect people the system usually ignores."

"And we have evidence," Lillian added, patting her medical bag. "Physical proof that can't be dismissed or intimidated."

Agent Loomis's modest brownstone in Brooklyn was dark when they arrived, but Mrs. Duval knocked with the authority of someone unaccustomed to being ignored. After several minutes, Loomis appeared at the door in his nightshirt and robe, looking understandably confused.

"Mrs. Duval? Miss Cross? What in God's name?"

"The Mulberry Street fire was arson," Lillian said without preamble. "William Hartley burned a tenement building to eliminate witnesses who could testify about his criminal activities. We have physical evidence, witness testimony, and a list of victims that connects directly to your investigation of Harrison Ashford's fraud network."

Loomis stared at them for a long moment, then stepped aside. "You'd better come in."

His parlor became an impromptu evidence examination room as Lillian spread out her samples and notes. Loomis studied everything with the meticulous attention of someone who'd built a career on thorough investigation, asking sharp questions and taking detailed notes.

"The accelerant samples alone prove arson," he said finally. "Combined with the burn pattern documentation and Mrs. Ferrante's eyewitness testimony about the two men in the basement, this is a strong case."

"Strong enough to stop the demolition?" Blackwood asked.

"Strong enough to secure the site as a federal crime scene." Loomis was already pulling on clothes, transforming from sleepy homeowner to federal agent with impressive speed. "I'll have agents at that building by dawn. The demolition crew will have to wait until we've finished our investigation."

"And the witnesses?" Rosa asked. "The families that Hartley has terrorized into silence?"

"Will receive federal protection starting immediately." Loomis's expression was grim. "Hartley made a mistake. Mass murder to intimidate witnesses isn't clever, it's desperation. And desperate men make mistakes."

As Loomis prepared to mobilize his federal resources, Lillian felt the familiar satisfaction of an investigation reaching its turning point. They'd found evidence, connected victims to motive, and secured official support for their case.

But William Hartley was still free, still dangerous, and now aware that they were pursuing him. The fight was far from over, and the most dangerous phase was just beginning.

The ashes of Mulberry Street had revealed their secrets. Now came the harder task, ensuring those secrets resulted in justice rather than more tragedy.

Dawn broke over Manhattan with the kind of cold clarity that made everything seem sharp-edged and unforgiving. Lillian stood at the window of Cross & Associates, watching the city wake while running on no sleep and too much coffee. Below, federal agents were already moving through the streets toward Mulberry Street, transforming what should have been a routine demolition into a federal crime scene.

Detective Blackwood returned from his brief trip home to change clothes, looking only marginally more rested than Lillian felt. "Agent Loomis's already at the site with eight investigators. They've cordoned off the entire block."

"How did Hartley react?"

"According to Loomis, he arrived thirty minutes

ago with his attorneys, demanding to know why federal agents were interfering with private property management." Blackwood's smile was grim. "Loomis showed him the warrant and suggested he might want to consult those attorneys about arson and murder charges."

"I wish I could have seen his face." Lillian turned from the window, feeling the weight of exhaustion beginning to catch up with her. "What about Rosa?"

"Mrs. Duval took her to the boarding house where Katherine Vandermeer stayed during the Ashford investigation. It's secure, and the landlady knows not to let anyone in without proper identification." Blackwood settled into the chair across from her desk. "We need to talk about what happens next."

"We testify at Harrison's trial and provide evidence linking Hartley to the fire," Lillian said, as if it were obvious.

"We also become visible targets for a man who's already killed thirty-seven people to protect his secrets." Blackwood's concern was evident. "Lillian, Hartley knows who we are, knows we're investigating him, and knows we've provided evidence to federal authorities. He's not going to wait passively for arrest."

Before Lillian could respond, rapid footsteps sounded on the stairs leading to their office. Mrs. Duval burst through the door, her usual composure cracked by obvious urgency.

"The trial," she said without warning. "Harrison's attorneys are requesting a delay. They're claiming that new evidence related to the Mulberry Street fire requires additional time to review and prepare a defense."

"That's absurd," Blackwood protested. "The fire has nothing to do with Harrison's fraud charges."

"Except that Harrison and Hartley were

business partners, and the fire eliminated witnesses who could have testified about their joint criminal activities." Mrs. Duval sank into a chair, her exhaustion matching theirs. "The defense is arguing that the prosecution has been coordinating with arson investigators to build a broader conspiracy case without providing adequate discovery to the defense."

"Which is technically true," Lillian admitted. "Morrison only connected the fire to Harrison's case a few hours ago."

"The judge is considering the motion this afternoon." Mrs. Duval pulled out a telegram. "Loomis sent this thirty minutes ago. He wants you both at the courthouse at two o'clock to provide testimony about the connection between the fire and the fraud conspiracy."

Lillian checked the clock, eight hours to prepare testimony that would need to connect two separate investigations, explain complex forensic evidence, and withstand aggressive cross-examination from attorneys who'd been paid very well to protect wealthy criminals.

"We need to document everything," she said, already moving toward her files. "Every connection between victims and Hartley's businesses, every piece of evidence linking the fire to witness intimidation, every reason the judge should deny the delay and proceed with the trial."

They spent the morning building their case, organizing evidence and preparing testimony. Mrs. Duval coordinated with Loomis's office, ensuring the federal investigators understood which specific witnesses had been eliminated and how their testimony would have damaged both Harrison and Hartley.

At one o'clock, as they were preparing to leave for the courthouse, a messenger arrived with a note addressed to Lillian. The handwriting was elegant, expensive, the kind taught in finishing schools that daughters of morticians never attended.

Miss Cross,

You've been quite industrious in your investigation of the unfortunate incident at Mulberry Street. However, you may want to consider whether pursuing this matter is worth the cost. Accidents happen to people who involve themselves in affairs beyond their understanding. Your father's funeral parlor, for instance, is located in a building with rather outdated fire safety measures. It would be tragic if something were to happen there.

A concerned observer

The threat was clear, the message unmistakable. Lillian's hands trembled as she showed it to Blackwood and Mrs. Duval.

"He's threatening your father," Blackwood said, his voice tight with anger. "And the funeral parlor, he's making it clear he'll burn another building if you testify."

"Then we ensure my father is protected and I testify anyway." Lillian's fear was transforming into fury. "Hartley thinks we'll back down because he's willing to kill. He's wrong."

"Lillian—"

"No." She met Blackwood's eyes with absolute determination. "Charlotte Vandermeer knew she was walking into danger when she confronted Harrison, but she did it anyway because the truth mattered. Thirty-seven people died in Hartley's fire. I won't let their deaths be meaningless because I was too frightened to testify."

Mrs. Duval was already at the door. "I'll have federal agents positioned at the funeral parlor within the hour. And I'll ensure your father understands the situation and takes appropriate precautions."

As they made their way to the courthouse, Lillian felt the familiar mixture of fear and purpose that had come to characterize her investigations. The powerful always believed their threats would work, that ordinary people would choose safety over justice. But every successful investigation began with someone deciding that truth mattered more than personal safety.

The courthouse was chaos. News of the arson charges and the connection to Harrison's fraud case had spread, drawing reporters, curious spectators, and representatives from immigrant rights organizations. Lillian spotted Alistair Penrose among the crowd, his notebook already open and his expression suggesting he smelled the story of the century.

"Miss Cross!" He approached quickly. "Is it true that William Hartley burned a tenement building to eliminate witnesses?"

"I can't comment on an ongoing investigation," Lillian replied, though she appreciated his presence. Penrose's coverage of the Charlotte Vandermeer case had helped force accountability. His reporting on the Mulberry Street fire could do the same.

"But you will be testifying this afternoon?"

"I will."

Penrose's smile was grim. "Then I'll make sure every paper in the city prints your testimony. Hartley can try to intimidate one witness, but he can't silence everyone."

Inside the courthouse, Agent Loomis briefed them on what to expect. "The defense will try to discredit your forensic analysis, question your qualifications, and suggest you're making wild accusations based on circumstantial evidence. Stay calm, stick to facts, and don't let them provoke you."

The courtroom was packed when they entered. Harrison Ashford sat at the defense table looking pale but composed, flanked by three expensive attorneys. In the gallery, Lillian spotted William Hartley, his expression carrying the confident arrogance of someone who'd never faced real consequences for his actions.

The judge, an older man with the severe expression of someone who'd seen every courtroom trick, called the hearing to order. "We're here to consider the defense's motion for a delay based on newly discovered evidence related to an arson investigation. Agent Loomis, you may present the prosecution's opposition to this motion."

Loomis stood, his federal credentials lending weight to his words. "Your Honor, the defense's motion is a transparent attempt to delay justice. The Mulberry Street fire isn't 'newly discovered evidence', it's a desperate act by one of the defendants' business associates to eliminate witnesses before they could testify."

The lead defense attorney, a silver-haired man whose suit probably cost more than Lillian earned in six months, rose with practiced indignation. "Your Honor, that's an inflammatory accusation without supporting evidence. My client has no connection to any fire, and suggesting otherwise without proof is prosecutorial misconduct."

"I have proof," Loomis countered, producing Lillian's forensic report. "Physical evidence of arson, witness testimony placing Mr. Hartley's associates at the scene, and documentation showing that multiple fire victims had knowledge of criminal activities involving both Mr. Ashford and Mr. Hartley."

"And who conducted this supposed forensic analysis?" the defense attorney asked. "A trained fire investigator? A federal expert? Or," he consulted his notes with obvious disdain, "a mortician's daughter who dabbles in detective work?"

"Miss Lillian Cross," Loomis said firmly, "who has assisted in solving two major criminal conspiracies, whose forensic analysis has been accepted as evidence in previous proceedings, and who risked her life last night to gather proof of arson and mass murder."

"Call your first witness," the judge instructed.

Lillian took the stand, feeling the weight of dozens of eyes, some sympathetic, some hostile, all measuring whether the daughter of a mortician had any right to testify in matters of such importance. She placed her hand on the Bible and swore to tell the truth, then settled into the witness chair with a composure she didn't entirely feel.

Loomis's questions were straightforward, allowing her to explain her examination of the fire scene, her collection of accelerant samples, and her analysis of burn patterns that proved the fire had been deliberately set. She described the physical evidence methodically, supporting each conclusion with specific observations.

Then came the cross-examination.

"Miss Cross," the defense attorney began, his tone dripping with condescension, "you claim to be qualified to conduct forensic analysis of a fire scene. What formal training do you have in fire investigation?"

"I have extensive experience in forensic examination through my work in my father's funeral parlor, and I've studied chemistry, anatomy, and investigative techniques—"

"But no formal training in fire investigation specifically," he interrupted. "No certification from any recognized authority. No academic credentials beyond what you've taught yourself."

"The evidence speaks for itself," Lillian replied calmly. "The accelerant samples, the burn patterns, the point of origin, these are objective facts that any qualified examiner would reach the same conclusions about."

"Or," the attorney suggested, "they're the misinterpretations of an amateur playing detective, seeing conspiracies where there are only accidents."

Before Lillian could respond, a commotion at the back of the courtroom drew everyone's attention. Fire Marshal O'Brien had entered, accompanied by two official fire investigators.

"Your Honor," O'Brien said, approaching the bench. "I apologize for the interruption, but I believe the court should hear from qualified fire investigators who've examined the Mulberry Street scene."

The judge looked annoyed but intrigued. "You have something relevant to add to these proceedings, Marshal?"

"We have confirmation of Miss Cross's findings. My investigators examined the site this morning at the request of federal authorities. Their analysis matches hers in every significant detail—the fire was deliberately set using paraffin-based accelerant, originated in the basement, and spread with a pattern consistent with arson rather than accident."

The defense attorney's confidence visibly faltered. "Your Honor, these investigators haven't been properly deposed—"

"Because the examination only concluded two hours ago," O'Brien interrupted. "But we have photographic evidence, chemical analysis, and professional documentation that corroborates everything Miss Cross has testified to."

As O'Brien's investigators took the stand and confirmed Lillian's forensic conclusions, she saw Hartley's expression shift from confidence to concern. The defense's strategy of attacking her credentials had backfired, now official investigators with impeccable qualifications were vouching for her analysis.

The judge listened to all the testimony, reviewed the evidence, and finally rendered his decision. "The defense's motion for delay is denied. The connection between the Mulberry Street fire and the current case is sufficiently established to proceed. Mr. Ashford's trial will continue as scheduled, and the prosecution may present evidence of Mr. Hartley's involvement in both the fraud conspiracy and the arson."

As the courtroom erupted in reaction, reporters rushing to file stories, defense attorneys huddling in urgent consultation, immigrant families in the gallery weeping with relief, Lillian felt the satisfaction of a major victory. They'd overcome attempts to discredit her testimony, secured official validation of their evidence, and ensured the trial would move forward.

But as she left the witness stand, she caught Hartley's eyes across the courtroom. The look he gave her was pure, undisguised hatred, the expression of a man who'd just realized he was going to lose everything.

And a man with nothing left to lose was the most dangerous kind of enemy.

The federal agents stationed outside Cross & Sons Funeral Parlor were a visible reminder that testifying against powerful criminals came with consequences. Lillian watched them through the window of her father's parlor, two men in plain clothes who weren't quite managing to look like ordinary passersby.

"They've been there since noon," Edmund observed, joining her at the window. "Agent Loomis assured me they're quite competent, though I confess their presence is…unsettling."

"Better unsettling than unprotected." Lillian turned from the window, noting the dark circles under her father's eyes. He'd aged in the past two days, the weight of being targeted because of his daughter's investigation evident in every line of his face. "Father, if you want me to stop—"

"Don't." Edmund's voice was firm. "Thirty-seven people died because William Hartley valued profit over human life. If testifying against him puts us at risk, so be it. Some things are worth the danger."

A knock at the door made them both tense, but it was only Detective Blackwood, arriving for their evening strategy session. He carried a telegram that he handed to Lillian immediately.

"From Agent Loomis. Harrison Ashford's attorneys have offered a plea bargain."

Lillian read quickly, her pulse quickening. "He'll testify against Hartley in exchange for a reduced sentence. Twenty years instead of life."

"Will the prosecutors accept?" Edmund asked.

"Loomis says they're considering it. Harrison's testimony could provide direct evidence of Hartley's involvement in the fraud conspiracy, which strengthens the case for the arson being part of a larger pattern of witness elimination." Blackwood settled into a chair, his exhaustion evident. "But it also means Hartley knows his former partner is about to turn on him. That makes him even more dangerous."

As if summoned by the mention of danger, Mrs. Duval arrived with news that confirmed their worst fears. "There's been another fire. A boarding house in the Bowery—the one where I'd placed Rosa Ferrante under protection."

Lillian's heart stopped. "Rosa?"

"Safe. The federal agents got her out before the fire spread. But the building is a total loss, and" Mrs. Duval's voice hardened, "the fire marshal's preliminary assessment suggests arson. Same accelerant pattern as Mulberry Street."

"Hartley's sending a message," Blackwood said grimly. "He can reach anyone, anywhere, regardless of federal protection."

"Then we end this now." Lillian was already moving, grabbing her coat and medical bag. "Where is Rosa?"

"Federal safe house in Brooklyn. Loomis has her under guard with three agents." Mrs. Duval caught Lillian's arm. "But Lillian, think about what you're proposing. If you go to her, you draw attention to the safe house location. You make yourself a target."

"I'm already a target. The question is whether I hide until Hartley's arrested or I use that to our advantage." Lillian's mind was racing through possibilities. "Hartley's desperate. Desperate men make mistakes. If we can force him into the open…"

"We also give him opportunity to eliminate his most dangerous opponents," Edmund interrupted. "Lillian, I understand your determination, but—"

A crash from downstairs cut him off, the sound of breaking glass, followed immediately by the acrid smell of smoke. The federal agents outside were already moving, shouting warnings, but the funeral parlor's ground floor was filling with smoke with terrifying speed.

"Fire!" Edmund moved toward the stairs, but Blackwood grabbed him.

"The smoke's too thick already. We need another way out."

They could hear the agents outside trying to break down the front door, but precious seconds were passing. Lillian remembered the layout of the building, her father's second-floor apartment had windows overlooking the alley, but it was a significant drop to the ground.

"The roof," she said, pointing to the narrow stairs that led to the attic. "Father's building connects to the neighboring structure. We can cross over."

They climbed quickly, the smoke following them

up the stairwell. The attic was cramped and dark, filled with old furniture and storage, but Lillian found the small window that opened onto the roof. The November evening was bitterly cold, and the roof tiles were slick with frost, but it beat burning alive.

Behind them, they could hear the fire spreading with unnatural speed, accelerant-fueled flames that were consuming the funeral parlor's wooden interior with horrifying efficiency. Edmund's life's work, decades of careful business building, was being destroyed by a criminal desperate to send a message.

The gap between their building and the next was perhaps four feet, manageable if you weren't terrified of heights and the roof wasn't covered in ice. Lillian went first, using the momentum of three running steps to clear the gap. She landed hard on the neighboring roof, her medical bag swinging wildly.

"Mrs. Duval, you're next!"

Mrs. Duval gathered her skirts with the practical determination of someone who'd faced worse challenges than jumping between buildings. She cleared the gap with surprising grace, landing beside Lillian with only a slight stumble.

Blackwood helped Edmund to the edge, but the older man hesitated. Below, they could hear shouting, the federal agents had broken through the front door and were calling for them.

"Father, now!"

Edmund jumped, but his foot slipped on the icy roof at the last moment. His trajectory was wrong, his momentum insufficient. Blackwood lunged, grabbing Edmund's wrist as the older man fell short of the neighboring building.

"I've got you!" Blackwood strained, his feet braced against the roof's edge. "Don't let go!"

Lillian and Mrs. Duval grabbed Blackwood, adding their weight to help him pull Edmund up. For several terrifying seconds, Edmund dangled between buildings, the alley three stories below and the fire raging behind them. But gradually, inch by inch, they hauled him onto the safety of the neighboring roof.

Behind them, flames were now visible through the attic window they'd escaped from. The funeral parlor—Edmund's legacy, Lillian's childhood home, was being consumed by Hartley's desperation.

They made their way across two more buildings before finding a fire escape that would take them safely to ground level. Federal agents found them in the alley, their relief at finding everyone alive evident despite their professional composure.

"The fire's being contained," one agent reported. "But the funeral parlor… I'm sorry, Mr. Cross. The damage is extensive."

Edmund stared back at the flames consuming his building, his expression hollow. "Everything. My records, my equipment, thirty years of work."

"Father…" Lillian began, but he shook his head.

"No. Don't apologize. You were right to investigate, right to testify. Hartley did this, not you." His voice grew stronger, anger replacing shock. "And now we're going to ensure he pays for every life he's destroyed."

Agent Loomis arrived within minutes, his fury barely controlled. "This was a coordinated attack. While Hartley's people were setting fire to the funeral parlor, another team hit three other locations—my office, Detective Blackwood's boarding house, and Mrs. Duval's townhouse. All arson, all using the same accelerant pattern."

"Was anyone hurt?" Lillian asked, dreading the answer.

"Minor injuries, smoke inhalation, but no fatalities. We got lucky, our surveillance caught the arsonists at two locations, and we have them in custody now." Looms's expression was grim. "They're already talking, trying to negotiate deals. Both admit they were hired by men connected to Hartley."

"Then we have him," Blackwood said.

"Not quite. The hired arsonists never met Hartley directly, they dealt with intermediaries who paid in cash and provided equipment. We can prove Hartley's associates were involved, but connecting him directly…" Loomis shook his head. "His attorneys will argue he knew nothing about it, that rogue business associates acted without his knowledge."

"Unless we can catch him in the act," Lillian said slowly, an idea forming. "Or force him to incriminate himself directly."

"What are you proposing?"

"A trap. We let Hartley think he's won, that he's successfully intimidated us into silence. Then when he moves to ensure we can't testify—"

"We catch him with federal agents as witnesses," Loomis finished, understanding dawning. "It's dangerous. If it goes wrong…"

"If it goes wrong, Hartley gets away with mass murder," Lillian interrupted. "Father, would you be willing to help?"

Edmund looked at the burning funeral parlor, at the decades of work being reduced to ash, and nodded. "What do you need me to do?"

Over the next hour, they refined their plan. Edmund would send a message to Hartley through intermediaries, claiming he wanted to negotiate—offering to convince Lillian not to testify in exchange for financial compensation and guarantee of safety. It was the kind of corruption that men like Hartley expected, the kind of compromise they believed everyone would eventually accept.

"He'll smell a trap," Blackwood warned.

"But he's also desperate," Loomis countered.

"And desperate men want to believe the easy solution will work. If Edmund's approach seems genuine enough, a father trying to protect his daughter after watching his life's work burn, Hartley might take the bait."

"Where do we arrange the meeting?" Mrs. Duval asked.

"Somewhere public enough that Hartley feels safe, but controlled enough that federal agents can position themselves without being obvious." Lillian considered their options. "What about the courthouse? Tomorrow morning, before the trial resumes. We're all supposed to be there anyway, it won't seem suspicious if Edmund shows up early to speak with Hartley."

"And the courthouse has excellent acoustics," Morrison added with a slight smile. "Federal agents positioned in adjacent rooms could hear every word of the conversation."

They sent the message through carefully chosen intermediaries, people known to have flexible ethics and loose connections to Hartley's network. The response came within two hours: Hartley would meet Edmund at the courthouse at seven o'clock the following morning, ninety minutes before the trial was scheduled to resume.

That night, Lillian couldn't sleep. She lay in the temporary room Mrs. Duval had arranged, staring at the ceiling and thinking about everything that could go wrong. If Hartley suspected a trap, he might not come. If he came but refused to incriminate himself, they'd have nothing. And if he came prepared for violence…

But thirty-seven people had died because Hartley valued profit over human life. Edmund's funeral parlor had burned because Hartley thought intimidation would work. Rosa's husband and baby son were dead because asking questions about criminal activity carried a death sentence.

Someone had to stand up to men like Hartley.

Someone had to prove that money and power didn't make you untouchable.

Tomorrow morning, they would find out if truth and courage were enough to overcome wealth and violence.

The trap was set. All that remained was to see whether the hunter would become the hunted.

The courthouse was cold and empty at six-thirty in the morning, its marble halls echoing with the footsteps of federal agents positioning themselves for the trap. Lillian stood in a small anteroom adjacent to the main corridor, watching through a carefully positioned mirror as Edmund took his place on a bench near the grand staircase, exactly where Hartley had specified for their meeting.

"Testing," Agent Loomis whispered into the recording device they'd concealed beneath Edmund's coat. His voice came through clearly in the listening room where Lillian, Blackwood, and three other agents waited. "Can you hear me, Mr. Cross?"

Edmund coughed once, their agreed-upon signal that he could hear them.

"Remember," Loomis continued quietly, "your

goal is to get him talking about the fires, the witness elimination, any connection to the Mulberry Street arson. Let him feel in control. Desperate men brag when they think they're winning."

Lillian watched her father through the mirror, seeing the tension in his shoulders despite his outwardly calm posture. Edmund Cross had spent thirty years maintaining careful neutrality, serving families without judgment or involvement in their conflicts. Now he was actively participating in a sting operation against one of Manhattan's most dangerous criminals.

"He's here," Blackwood said quietly, pointing to the courthouse's main entrance.

William Hartley entered alone, his expensive overcoat and confident bearing suggesting a man without concerns. But Lillian noticed the way his eyes constantly scanned his surroundings, the tension in his movements that betrayed awareness of potential danger. He was suspicious, but not suspicious enough to stay away.

Hartley approached Edmund slowly, maintaining distance until the last moment. "Mr. Cross. I was somewhat surprised to receive your message."

"I imagine you were." Edmund's voice was steady, tired, the perfect tone of a man who'd been broken by violence and wanted only to salvage what remained. "My funeral parlor burned last night. Thirty years of work, destroyed in minutes."

"I heard. Tragic. These old buildings are such fire hazards." Hartley sat on the bench, leaving a careful space between them. "But surely you didn't ask for this meeting just to discuss your losses."

"I wanted to discuss my daughter's testimony." Edmund looked down at his hands, and Lillian recognized it as the gesture he used when delivering difficult news to grieving families, a carefully constructed vulnerability. "She's planning to testify about the Mulberry Street fire this afternoon. I'd like to convince her not to."

Hartley's expression didn't change, but Lillian saw interest spark in his eyes. "And why would you want that?"

"Because I've already lost my business. I don't want to lose my daughter as well." Edmund's voice carried just the right note of defeated pragmatism. "You've made your point, Mr. Hartley. People who oppose you suffer consequences. I understand that now."

"Do you?" Hartley leaned back slightly, his confidence growing. "And what exactly do you think you understand?"

"That the Mulberry Street fire wasn't an accident. That witnesses who could damage your business interests tend to meet unfortunate ends. That my daughter's investigation threatens you enough that you're willing to burn buildings and kill people to stop her." Edmund met Hartley's eyes. "I understand all of that. What I need to understand is what price you're willing to pay to make this go away."

In the listening room, Loomis tensed. This was the critical moment, would Hartley take the bait and incriminate himself, or would he recognize the trap and walk away?

Hartley was quiet for a long moment, studying Edmund with the calculating assessment of a predator evaluating prey. "You want money. Compensation for your destroyed business, assurances of future safety."

"I want my daughter alive and unharmed. Everything else is negotiable." Edmund's voice carried the exhaustion of genuine emotion, fear for his daughter mixing with the performance of a desperate father. "But I need to know that if Lillian withdraws her testimony, you'll leave us alone. No more fires, no more threats, no more accidents."

"Your daughter's testimony is problematic," Hartley admitted, his guard lowering slightly. "She's connected the Mulberry Street fire to witness elimination in a way that's… inconvenient. Her forensic analysis, combined with that Italian woman's eyewitness account, creates difficulties."

"Difficulties that murder can solve?" Edmund's tone was neutral, not accusatory, just a man seeking clarity about the rules of the game.

Hartley's smile was cold. "Murder is such an ugly word. I prefer to think of it as… managing liabilities. The Mulberry Street building had several residents who possessed inconvenient knowledge. The fire eliminated those liabilities while sending a message to others who might consider cooperating with federal investigators."

Lillian's breath caught. He was confessing, actually admitting to mass murder with the casual tone of someone discussing business strategy. In the listening room, Loomis was already signaling to agents positioned throughout the courthouse.

"Thirty-seven people," Edmund said quietly. "Families, children. All liabilities to be managed?"

"All obstacles to be removed." Hartley's arrogance was fully engaged now, the confidence of someone who'd gotten away with murder and believed he'd continue to do so. "Your daughter seems to think that forensic evidence and moral outrage will bring me to justice. But she doesn't understand how the world actually works. I have resources, connections, attorneys who know how to make inconvenient evidence disappear."

"Like you made the witnesses disappear?"

"Exactly. Though I'll admit, Harrison's cowardice in offering to testify against me is… disappointing. We built that network together, eliminated threats together. His betrayal will be addressed once the trial concludes." Hartley stood, apparently satisfied with the conversation. "So, Mr. Cross, here's my offer: your daughter withdraws her testimony, claims her forensic analysis was mistaken, and I'll ensure she lives to regret her interference rather than dying like those Mulberry Street residents. You'll receive fifty thousand dollars to rebuild your funeral parlor, and we'll all move forward."

"And if she refuses?"

Hartley's expression turned glacial. "Then I'll arrange for her to have an accident. A tragic fire, perhaps, or a fall from a great height. These things happen to people who persist in making trouble. You've seen what I'm willing to do to protect my interests. Don't doubt that I'll extend that same… efficiency… to dealing with your daughter."

"That's enough." Loomis's voice echoed through the corridor as federal agents emerged from concealed positions. "William Hartley, you're under arrest for conspiracy to commit murder, arson, and conspiracy to intimidate witnesses."

Hartley's face went white as he realized what had happened. He spun toward Edmund, fury replacing his earlier confidence. "You wore a wire. You tricked me into—"

"Into confessing to mass murder," Edmund said, his defeated posture vanishing. "Yes, I did. For my daughter, for Rosa Ferrante's family, and for thirty-seven people who died because you valued profit over human life."

Hartley lunged toward Edmund, but Blackwood was faster, intercepting him and forcing him to the ground. "That's enough out of you," Blackwood said with obvious satisfaction as he secured Hartley's wrists with iron cuffs. "Though that's rather ironic given how much you just said."

As federal agents took custody of Hartley

Lillian emerged from the listening room. She approached her father, who looked simultaneously relieved and shaken by what he'd done.

"Father—"

"Don't apologize," Edmund said firmly, pulling her into an embrace. "We did what needed to be done. Justice required risk, and I was willing to take it."

Agent Loomis joined them, holding the recording device that had captured every word of Hartley's confession. "This is ironclad. Admission of arson, conspiracy to commit murder, witness intimidation, and direct threats against Miss Cross. Combined with the forensic evidence, the testimony from the captured arsonists, and Harrison's pending testimony, Hartley is finished."

"What about the trial?" Lillian asked.

"Harrison Ashford's trial will proceed this afternoon. And based on what we just recorded, we'll be filing charges against Hartley for thirty-seven counts of murder, multiple counts of arson, and conspiracy charges that will ensure he never sees freedom again." Loomis's satisfaction was evident. "You've exposed one of the most extensive criminal conspiracies in Manhattan's history."

As the courthouse began filling with morning staff and early arrivals for the trial, word of Hartley's arrest spread rapidly. Reporters who'd been covering the Ashford case rushed to document this new development, their questions creating chaos in the normally sedate marble halls.

Alistair Penrose found Lillian amid the confusion. "Is it true? Hartley confessed to the Mulberry Street fire?"

"You'll have to ask Agent Loomis about official statements," Lillian replied, but her smile confirmed everything Penrose needed to know.

"This is going to be the biggest story of the

year," Penrose said, already scribbling notes. "Wealthy real estate developer exposed as arsonist and mass murderer. The whole rotten system of tenement exploitation laid bare." He looked up from his notebook. "Miss Cross, you've done it again. Another seemingly untouchable criminal brought to justice."

But Lillian was watching Rosa Ferrante, who'd arrived under federal escort for the day's proceedings. The young widow stood apart from the chaos, her expression a mixture of relief and grief that no justice could fully address.

"Mrs. Ferrante." Lillian approached her gently. "We got him. Hartley confessed to setting the fire."

"I heard." Rosa's voice was quiet. "They told me everything. He admitted killing Carlo and Antonio like it was nothing more than… what did he call it? Managing liabilities?"

"I'm so sorry. I know that hearing how casually he dismissed their lives—"

"No." Rosa straightened her shoulders with visible effort. "I needed to hear it. I needed to know that he understood exactly what he did and chose to do it anyway. Because now when they hang him—and they will hang him, won't they?"

"The evidence is overwhelming," Morrison confirmed, joining their conversation. "He'll face multiple death sentences for the Mulberry Street fire alone."

"Good." Rosa's voice carried steel beneath the grief. "Carlo always said that evil only wins when good people do nothing. He'd be proud that we stood up, that we fought back, that we made sure Hartley couldn't hurt anyone else."

As the morning progressed and the trial preparations continued, Lillian reflected on how the investigation had transformed. It had started with a telegram about a suspicious fire and evolved into exposing a conspiracy of fraud, intimidation, and mass murder. Charlotte Vandermeer's case had taught her that pursuing justice required courage. The Mulberry Street fire had taught her that sometimes courage meant risking everything you'd built.

Edmund's funeral parlor was destroyed, but they'd saved countless future victims. Hartley's wealth and connections hadn't protected him from his own arrogance. And thirty-seven people who'd died in flames would have their deaths answered with accountability.

"Miss Cross?" Mrs. Duval appeared at her elbow, as perfectly composed as if the past week's chaos hadn't affected her at all. "The trial is about to begin. They're calling you as their first witness."

The courtroom was packed, standing room only, with reporters filling every available space. Harrison Ashford sat at the defense table looking resigned to his fate, while the recently-vacated chair beside him stood as testament to his former partner's arrest.

Lillian took the stand and swore to tell the truth, then began her testimony about the forensic evidence connecting Hartley to the fire. But this time, her words carried the weight of Hartley's own confession, the validation of official fire investigators, and the moral authority of someone who'd risked everything for justice.

When she finished, the prosecution rested its case with a confidence that came from having built an unassailable argument. The defense attorneys conferred briefly, then declined to cross-examine.

"Your Honor," the lead defense attorney said wearily, "in light of Mr. Hartley's arrest and the evidence presented, my client wishes to revise his plea. Mr. Ashford will plead guilty to all charges in exchange for the previously discussed sentencing agreement."

As Harrison Ashford stood to formally enter his

guilty plea, Lillian caught Katherine Vandermeer's eye in the gallery. Charlotte's sister had come to witness justice for her own case, and now she was seeing justice delivered for thirty-seven more victims of the same criminal network.

The judge accepted the plea, set sentencing for the following month, and adjourned the proceedings. As the courtroom emptied, Lillian felt the familiar satisfaction of a case successfully concluded, tempered by the knowledge of what it had cost and whom it had hurt.

"It's over," Blackwood said, appearing at her side as they left the courthouse into the cold November afternoon.

"This case is over," Lillian corrected. "But there will be others. There are always others."

"And you'll investigate them," Blackwood said, not a question.

"Someone has to." Lillian looked back at the courthouse where justice had been delivered. "Someone has to speak for the dead and fight for the vulnerable. That's what we do."

As they made their way through the streets toward their temporary office, the funeral parlor would take months to rebuild, Lillian thought about the journey from mortician's daughter to private investigator. She'd learned to read the stories written in death, to pursue truth despite opposition, and to risk safety for justice.

Charlotte Vandermeer, thirty-seven Mulberry Street residents, and countless other victims had received justice because someone had refused to accept that the powerful were untouchable.

It was enough. For today, it was enough.

THE
RESURRECTION
MEN
by
JOLENE SKVAREK

# CHAPTER ONE:

## THE WEIGHT OF ABSENCE

The dead, as a rule, stayed where you put them.

This was, Lillian Cross had always believed, the fundamental contract between the living and the departed, a silent agreement, unwritten and absolute, that once the arrangements had been made and the certificates signed and the earth turned over, all parties would honor their respective positions. The living grieved. The dead remained. It was not a complicated arrangement. It had been functioning reliably, in Lillian's experience, since the first human being had the wit to bury another.

But then came the November of 1887, and the body of Mr. Gerald Pomeroy disappeared from its temporary holding vault sometime between ten o'clock on a Tuesday night and six o'clock on a Wednesday morning, and the contract was broken entirely.

Lillian learned of it at seven in the morning, standing in the muddy lot on Mulberry Street where Cross &

Sons Funeral Parlor had stood for twenty-three years before William Hartley's men had reduced it to charred timber and ash three weeks prior. The November air tasted of coal smoke and river damp and the particular mineral cold of a city that had been rained on and had not quite dried out. She had been at the site since five, supervising the carpenters her father had hired from the Dolan Brothers firm on Canal Street, watching the skeletal frame of the new building rise against a pewter sky. It was the kind of work that required her physical presence not because she understood carpentry, she was honest with herself about this, but because Edmund Cross was recovering from a bruised rib and a wrenched shoulder sustained during the events preceding the Ashford trial, and because the Dolan Brothers had a tendency, when left unsupervised, to make decisions that prioritized their schedule over the client's specifications.

Three days ago she had caught them framing the preparation room doorway six inches narrower than the plans called for. Yesterday they had attempted to site the cold storage vault on the south wall rather than the north, which would have rendered it functionally useless in summer. This morning she had arrived to find them debating, in a collegial and completely unauthorized way, whether the second-floor storage room was strictly necessary or whether the space might be better used as an extension of the main parlor.

The second-floor storage room was not optional. She had explained this at some length.

She had been in the middle of explaining it again, with the aid of the original architectural drawings spread across a makeshift table of sawhorses and planks, when the boy appeared at the edge of the lot.

He was perhaps twelve, with the gap-toothed directness of a child raised on the lower streets, where the fastest way to get something done was to say it plainly and save the ceremony for people who had time for it. He pushed through the loose ring of carpenters without hesitation and addressed himself to Lillian with the evaluating look of someone who had been given a description and was checking it against the reality.

"You Miss Cross? The undertaker lady?"

"That description is adequate," Lillian said.

"Detective Blackwood says you should come to the Calvary Street vault. Says to come now." The boy scrunched his face, recalling the exact phrasing with the conscientiousness of someone who had been told it mattered. "Says you'll want to see this before anyone else does, and that he's already waited longer than he should have."

Lillian looked at the boy and then at the architectural drawings and then at the head carpenter, a broad-faced man named Kolb who had been in the trade for thirty years and who regarded her with the particular expression of a man who had not previously been managed by a woman in her mid-twenties and was still deciding how he felt about it.

"The storage room stays as drawn," she said. "The doorframe measurements are in the top margin of the plan. If there is a deviation from those measurements by the time I return, we will be having a different conversation about the remainder of this contract."

Kolb opened his mouth.

"Thank you, Mr. Kolb," Lillian said, and followed the boy north through the gray morning.

✦ ✦ ✦

Mulberry Street in November had a particular quality that Lillian had grown up with and could no longer see quite objectively. She had lived within four blocks of it her entire life, had walked it in every season and every weather, had known it when the elevated train was new and when the gaslight replaced the oil lamps and when the tenements went up on the east side of the street and changed the light in a way that took her a year to stop noticing. She knew the way the pushcart vendors arranged themselves by unspoken agreement, the fish sellers on the east side in the morning because the smell went west with the prevailing wind, the dry goods carts clustering near the corner where foot traffic was heaviest. She knew which buildings had ground-floor businesses that kept their doors open in cold weather and which had superintendents who enforced the opposite policy. She knew the bakery on the corner of Hester that put yesterday's bread out at six in the morning and was sold out by seven.

She knew it, in other words, the way you knew a place that had shaped you before you were old enough to choose it. And she knew, walking north through it now, that it was watching the rebuilding of Cross & Sons with the complicated attention of a neighborhood that had opinions.

The opinions were not all favorable.

The Hartley affair had been in the papers for three weeks. The arson was established fact, and the thirty-seven deaths in the Mulberry Street tenement fire were being prosecuted as murder. But newspapers required villains and complications in roughly equal measure, and the complications had included, in two separate articles, references to the Cross family's role in the investigation, references that were admiring in their intent and somewhat damaging in their effect. The neighborhood understood, now, that the undertaker's daughter had been involved in bringing down a powerful man. Some of them thought this was admirable. Some of them thought it was exactly the kind of thing that brought trouble down on a block, and that trouble, when it came, was not selective about whose door it knocked on.

Three of her father's regular clients had sent polite notes declining to renew their arrangements with Cross

& Sons. Two new families had come in, specifically asking for the firm that had pursued justice for the Mulberry Street dead. Lillian kept both sets of correspondence in a folder she had labeled, with deliberate neutrality, "Ongoing."

The Calvary Street vault was twenty minutes north on foot, situated in a hillside that had been carved into with the practical-minded ingenuity of a city that needed to put bodies somewhere when the ground was too frozen to bury them. The surrounding streets were quieter than the lower neighborhoods, fewer vendors, fewer children, the traffic more deliberate. Institutions tended to collect here: a church, a charitable hospital, a school for immigrant children that had been founded by a Quaker society and was perpetually six months from insolvency. The vault itself was not signposted. People who needed to find it generally knew where it was.

Detective Blackwood was waiting at the iron gate.

He was leaning against the gatepost with his arms crossed and his coat collar turned up against the cold, and when Lillian came through the gate he straightened with the movement of a man who had been still for a while and was glad to have a reason to stop. He had a look she had learned to read in the months since the Hartley investigation began, a particular quality of contained attention that meant he had already assessed the situation, had already formed a preliminary view, and was now waiting to see whether her assessment would confirm or complicate his own.

She had catalogued his expressions with the same methodical attention she gave to physical evidence. It was, she had decided, a purely professional interest. The decision required occasional maintenance.

"Blackwood," she said. "Tell me."

"Good morning to you as well." He gestured for the vault keeper, a small, distressed man named Hutchins who had the look of someone who had been awake since four and was now questioning the choices that had brought him to this moment, to open the gate. "Gerald Pomeroy, age sixty-three. Admitted eleven days ago following death by stroke, certified by Dr. Hartenstein on the fourteenth. Family notified of interment date for the seventeenth, contingent on the arrival of a son traveling from Boston."

"I know all of this," Lillian said. "I arranged the storage myself."

"I know you did. I'm establishing the record." He held the gate for her with a slight inclination of his head that was not quite ceremony and not quite irony. "When Hutchins arrived at six this morning to perform his routine welfare check, vault three was empty."

Lillian looked at Hutchins. He looked at a point approximately three feet to the left of her.

"Define empty," she said.

"The body is gone. The shroud is gone. The identification card remains in the brass holder on the door." Blackwood's voice was level, but she had learned to hear what lived underneath the level tone. Something about this particular situation was bothering him beyond the professional disturbance of a missing body. "I've already sent a man to inform the Pomeroy family. The son arrived from Boston yesterday afternoon."

The son arrived from Boston yesterday afternoon. Lillian absorbed this and set it in the part of her mind she kept for facts that required feeling later, when the work was done.

"Who else knows?" she asked.

"Hutchins, myself, and the two officers I brought with me to secure the site. I sent them away before you arrived." He paused. "I wanted you to see it first."

She stepped inside.

The vault was a stone room, twelve feet square and perhaps eight feet high, carved directly into the hillside so that the earth pressed against three walls and the temperature inside remained within a few degrees of freezing regardless of the weather outside. Iron shelving units lined the east and west walls, currently empty. The north wall held six narrow niches cut into the stone itself, each sealed with a hinged iron door approximately two feet wide and four feet tall, fitted with a simple latch and a brass name-card holder at eye level. Five of the holders bore cards. The sixth, vault three, counting left to right, was empty, and its door stood a precise six inches open.

Not broken open. Not forced. Open in the deliberate way of a door unlatched by hand and left ajar, either in carelessness or as a kind of punctuation.

Lillian examined the latch. Clean mechanism, no scratches on the surrounding iron. She crouched and looked at the floor in front of the niche, stone flags, slightly dusty, with a disturbance in the dust consistent with something heavy being slid out horizontally. The disturbance ran from the niche to approximately the center of the room.

"Who holds keys to this facility?" she asked, without looking up.

Hutchins cleared his throat. "Myself. The Board of Health overseer, Mr. Fenn, who holds a master key for all six municipal vaults in the district. And —" He stopped.

"And?"

"The undertaking establishments with clients currently in storage. Standard practice, they require access for professional purposes, to check on their —"

"Which establishments?"

A pause. "At present, two. Whitfield & Sons on Hester Street, who have a Mrs. Clara Sutton in vault one. And Cross and Sons." He did not look at her. "Your father holds the key, miss. It was registered to Edmund Cross when the storage arrangement was made two weeks ago."

Lillian stood. She was aware of Blackwood watching her from the doorway, aware of the quality of his attention, not anticipatory, not waiting for a particular reaction. Simply present. Witnessing.

"It looks," she said, after a moment in which she assembled several things into a workable order, "like someone wants it to look a particular way." She turned to Blackwood. "I want to see the exterior. All of it."

He nodded. He said nothing about the key, nothing about her father's name in the registry. She filed this as something to return to.

Outside, the morning had lightened enough to work with. Lillian moved around the building systematically, starting at the front entrance and working clockwise, covering the ground in the careful grid she'd developed over years of reading scenes that the police had either already disturbed or not yet thought to examine. The front presented nothing. The east wall, pressed against the hillside, presented nothing. The south wall had a coal delivery chute, sealed with a padlock that had not been touched recently.

The north wall was a different matter.

Below the single narrow window set high in the stone, a ventilation window, not large enough to admit a person, the ground was soft from two days of light rain. And in the softness, beginning approximately four feet from the wall and running in a straight line toward the road, there were marks.

She crouched and looked at them without touching anything.

Not footprints, or not primarily. The footprints were there, at least three distinct sets, she thought, heavy-soled working boots, but they were overlaid on and around a series of parallel drag lines, each approximately eighteen inches wide, spaced three or four feet apart. The drag lines ran clean and deliberate through the soft ground, the way something heavy moved by men who knew what they were doing would run.

Three sets.

She looked up at Blackwood, who had come around the corner and was crouching a few feet away, examining the same evidence with the same quality of careful attention.

"They didn't only take Pomeroy," she said.

He was already nodding, slowly. "I know. I checked the other vaults before you arrived. Mrs. Sutton, from Whitfield's, is gone from vault one. And an unclaimed man admitted five days ago, a canal accident, no identification, is gone from vault five." He paused. "I didn't tell Hutchins I'd noticed. He hasn't checked."

Three bodies. Three sets of drag lines running toward the road, where the ground was churned with the marks of a carriage standing still for some minutes and then moving.

"Resurrection men," Lillian said. The words had a particular flatness in the cold morning air. Body snatching, the theft of cadavers for sale to anatomists and medical schools — had been a feature of city life for as long as cities had had medical schools, which was to say for as long as anyone currently living could remember. The Anatomy Act of 1854 had been designed to address the shortage of legal teaching material by expanding access to unclaimed bodies, and it had worked, in the way that legislation generally worked against established economic incentives: imperfectly and unevenly, leaving a black market that was smaller than it had been and more discreet, but not gone.

"A professional operation," Blackwood said. "Not opportunists. Someone who knew which bodies were here, knew which ones would be noticed quickly and which wouldn't, and came with the equipment and the manpower to move three in a single night." He looked at her steadily. "Someone who had access to the intake records or to someone who did."

"Or who had a key."
"Yes."
The word sat between them in the cold air. Lillian looked at the drag lines and thought about what it meant to know, specifically, that Gerald Pomeroy was in vault three. The Board of Health kept intake records. Hutchins kept intake records. The undertakers with clients in storage knew their own clients. But Pomeroy was a Cross & Sons client, and the only Cross & Sons key in the registry was registered to Edmund Cross.

She was aware that this was the shape of a trap, and that recognizing the shape of a trap and being able to step out of it were not the same thing.

"I'll need to see the Board of Health intake records," she said. "The full registry of key holders, not just current ones. Anyone who has held a key to this facility in the past year."

"I've already requested them." He said it matter-of-factly, as though this were the natural order of things, which perhaps it was. "I've also put in a request to speak with Fenn this afternoon. He approves access applications personally."

"And the Pomeroy son?"

A slight pause. "I'll handle that conversation myself, if you'd prefer."

Lillian thought about the son who had come from Boston for a burial and had instead arrived at a city in which his father's body was somewhere unknown. She thought about what that felt like, and then she set the feeling aside in the same part of her mind as before.

"We'll handle it together," she said. "But not today. Today I need information before I can give him anything useful." She straightened and brushed the cold mud from her coat. "I'm going to speak to my father's colleague — the one who arranged the vault access. And I'll visit Mrs. Duval. If there's a body trade operating in this neighborhood with enough organization to hit a municipal vault, she'll have heard something."

"I'll meet you at the office when I have the Board records." He caught himself. "The construction site."

Something that was almost a smile moved through Lillian's expression and was gone. "Kolb is probably using the time to redesign the second floor," she said.

Blackwood looked at her in that particular way — not quite warm, not quite professional, balanced precisely between the two in a place that had been expanding gradually over the past weeks. She had noticed the expansion. She had not yet decided what to do with the noticing.

"I'll find you there," he said.

She went to find a cab. Behind her she heard Hutchins beginning, belatedly and with considerable distress, to check the other vaults.

BOOK 2
OF
THE UNDERTAKER'S DAUGHTER
RESURRECTION MEN
COMING SOON

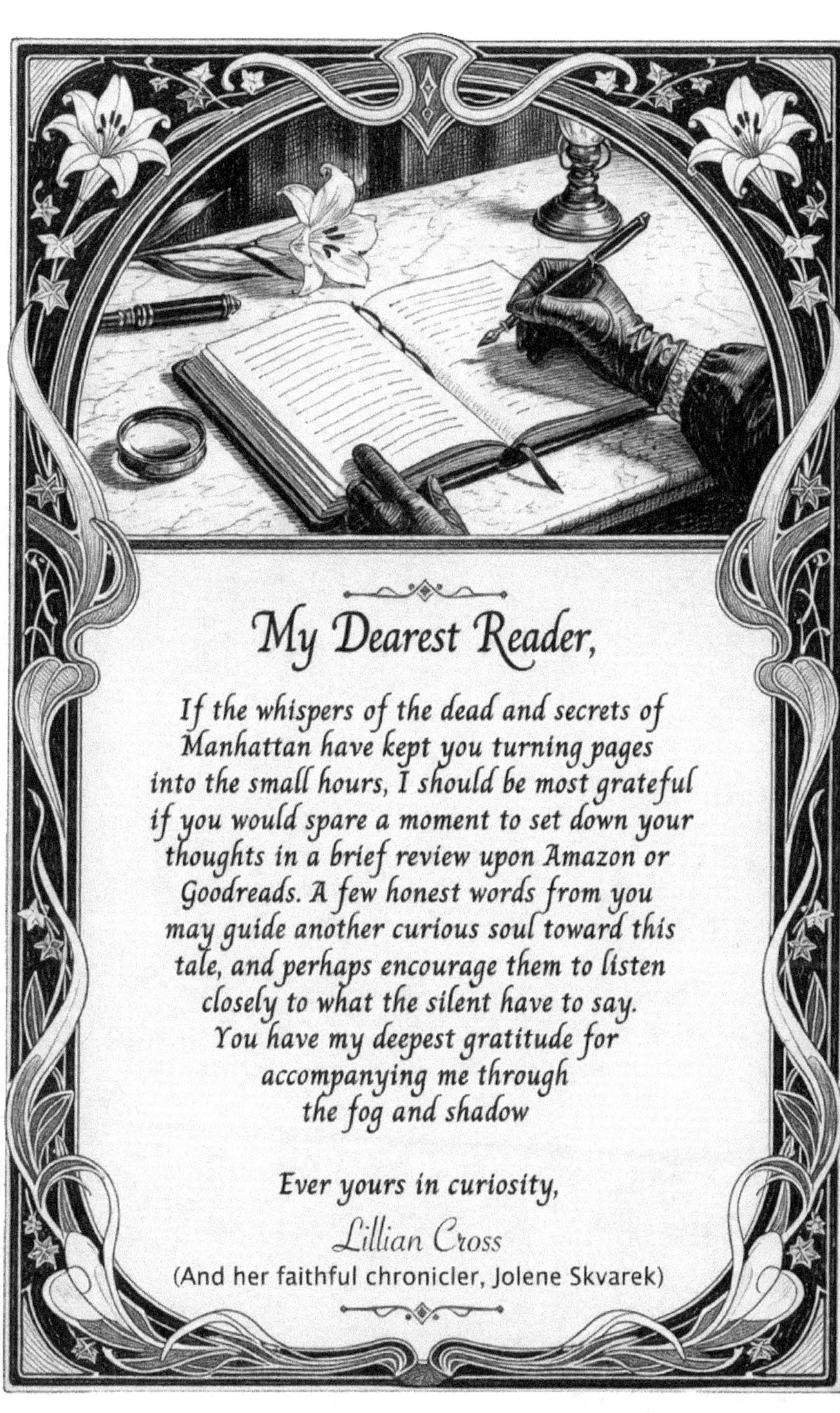

## My Dearest Reader,

*If the whispers of the dead and secrets of Manhattan have kept you turning pages into the small hours, I should be most grateful if you would spare a moment to set down your thoughts in a brief review upon Amazon or Goodreads. A few honest words from you may guide another curious soul toward this tale, and perhaps encourage them to listen closely to what the silent have to say. You have my deepest gratitude for accompanying me through the fog and shadow*

*Ever yours in curiosity,*

*Lillian Cross*

(And her faithful chronicler, Jolene Skvarek)

www.ingramcontent.com/pod-product-compliance
Lightning Source LLC
LaVergne TN
LVHW010646110826
845149LV00014B/2973

* 9 7 9 8 9 9 3 3 3 4 5 1 6 *